A LIFE TRANSPARENT

A LIFE TRANSPARENT

TODD KEISLING

This book is a work of fiction. Names, characters, places, and incidents either are the product of the author's imagination or are used fictitiously and any resemblance to actual persons, living or dead, business establishments, events, or locales is entirely coincidental.

A LIFE TRANSPARENT
Copyright © 2007 by Todd Keisling
Second Paperback Edition: January 2011

All rights reserved. No part of this book may be reproduced or transmitted in any form or by any means, electronic or mechanical, including photocopying, recording, or by any information storage and retrieval system, without permission in writing from the author, except by a reviewer who may quote brief passages in review.

ISBN 978-0-9830019-1-1
LCCN 2010941696

Published by Precipice Books

Cover design and author photo by Erica Keisling

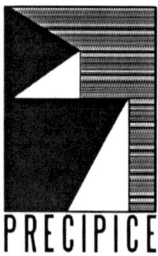

http://www.precipicebooks.com

For Erica

A LIFE TRANSPARENT

–PROLOGUE–
THIS BANAL COIL

A℠ Sᴘᴀʀʀᴏᴡ ᴅɪᴅɴ'ᴛ know the man, which made him easier to kill. Smith huddled near the mouth of the alley, his dirty paws reaching out in supplication to the people passing by. Sparrow admired Smith's humility even though it would profit him nothing. The man controlling them made it clear: the populace was unable to see them.

"Spare some change?"

Smith's pleas fell on deaf ears. Lunchtime crowds raced down the sidewalks, busy with daily tasks and self-importance. The smell from a pizzeria across the street carried over, displacing the funk of garbage and exhaust fumes.

Sparrow lifted his tired face to the sunlight, basking in its simple radiance. He licked the air with his tongue, tasting its intricacies. Every moment of freedom from the gray was a cherished blessing. He couldn't remember how long he'd been trapped there, or what today's date was. Fortunately, it wouldn't matter for much longer, not after he'd done what he had to do.

"Anyone? Change for food? Haven't eaten for days."

Sparrow tried to ignore Smith's grating pleas, busying himself with the task at hand. He knelt beside the dumpster and shoved his arm into the dark gap underneath. His fingers blindly searched through the grime that blanketed the alley floor. Where was it? His heart rate rose with nervous fervor. This would be his salvation, and he would have only one chance to do it.

Thoughts of their warden, the Gatekeeper of the Gray, filled him with adrenaline. He would not go back. Not to the fate that awaited him. The master had plans for him. Grand plans. He could hear that monotone voice in his head, booming: *We will shuffle you off your banal coil, Mr. Sparrow, and it will be glorious.*

Sparrow's searching fingers finally skated over the blade. He smiled, pulling the knife from its hiding place. The warden had little control in this colorful void.

"Mister? Coins for a sorry soul?"

Albert Sparrow climbed to his feet, brushing away the grime from his clothing. He took a breath, listening to his heartbeat, and tasting sweet murder on his tongue. Smith continued his futile begging, oblivious to Sparrow's slow advance toward the mouth of the alley.

Overhead, the sky dimmed. The cars which crowded the street began to fade from view. The people on the sidewalks were as transparent outlines, ghosts wandering a desolate painting of civilization. Sparrow gripped the knife. It was dull, the blade spotted with rust. He stood behind Smith.

"They can't hear you," Sparrow said.

"I can try," Smith said, offering his companion a fleeting glance before his attention returned to the street. The world lightened, flooded once again with color. Cars and people returned in full form. "There's always hope I can change things."

Sparrow raised the blade, but hesitated. He almost pitied the man. "We made our choices. Some of us belong here."

Smith scoffed. "Easy for you to say. You've got his favor. The rest of us are going to rot." He pulled back his sleeve, revealing pale flesh marked with clusters of gray pox. "Bastard's sucking us dry."

Nothing ventured, he thought. He sliced the air in a short arc, plunging the rusted blade deep into the man's back. *Nothing gained.*

Smith let out a rattling gasp. He turned, eyes wide in shock, one hand grasping for the weapon. In an act of twisted benevolence Sparrow helped him withdraw the knife, gritting his teeth as blood flowed from the wound.

"*Why*—"

Sparrow again thrust himself upon the man and pressed the blade against his throat.

"Sorry, friend. You're my ticket out. I figure murder is random enough to break the strings." He put force against the handle, inching the blade into Smith's neck. Sparrow watched as life left the man's eyes: they dilated, lost focus, and finally went blank. Smith gurgled one final breath. Blood gushed from the wound.

He let go of the knife and stumbled backward—it was done. The sky dimmed, and the world flashed gray. He felt a force wrenching at his stomach, threatening to tear it from him, but after a moment it relented. Crowds and traffic reappeared. Sparrow sucked in the air as if for the first time.

Sparrow calmed himself, methodically wiping Smith's blood on his pant leg before walking out of the alleyway toward traffic.

The voice coming from behind him was unmistakable—the warden, his master. In the gray world it would've boomed across the heavens, through the very fibers of his being. Here in the real world, full of its wonderful colors and depth, his master's voice was but a whisper on the breeze, a tickle at the back of his neck.

You are breaking the rules, Mr. Sparrow.

But Sparrow was running, and he would not look back.

-1-
A LIFE ORDINARY

Donovan Candle's alarm sounded at 6:30 AM. He stirred in his sleep, eyes fluttering behind their lids as the blaring noise rose in waves of stabbing intensity. He struggled to keep himself wrapped in the warmth of sleep, treading the peaceful waters of an otherwise vivid dream.

Donna's elbow promptly connected with his ribs. His eyes flew open, and his hand found the alarm. After switching it off, Donovan rose, saw the time, and frowned. He'd already lost two minutes of his morning.

He was careful not to disturb Donna, whose alarm was set to wake her at 6:45. She justified those fifteen minutes, saying she needed them on account of beauty rest, and he didn't argue with her. Donovan paused at the door and looked over at her sleeping face. He smiled, and made his way to the bathroom.

An unsettling feeling rose suddenly within the pit of his stomach. It caught him off guard, a sensation that felt like clammy fingers curling around his insides, tugging. He put a hand to his belly and waited for it to pass.

What the hell was that? he wondered. The sensation relented, giving way to a low rumble of hunger. It was still a while before breakfast, and so he busied himself with a shower and shave.

Donna was awake when he finished, as evidenced by the sound of the coffee maker gurgling downstairs. The scent of frying eggs made his stomach growl. He went to the bedroom, saw the time was 6:53, and began to dress in his Monday clothes: a dark green Oxford, khakis, black belt, and matching shoes tied left foot first. His watch struck 7:00 as he fastened its band. He smiled. *Right on schedule*, he thought, and wandered downstairs for breakfast.

Donna greeted him with bleary eyes, a tender smile, and a kiss. He poured himself a cup of coffee, took a seat at the table, and folded a napkin on his lap. That odd pull in his stomach resurfaced briefly, but he forgot it as Donna brought over the frying pan and served his eggs.

"Thanks, hon."

"There's bacon on the stove, too." She returned to the counter and placed the pan in the sink.

"Aren't you going to eat?"

Two pieces of toast popped out of the toaster. Donna tossed them onto a plate and returned to the table. "I'm starting a diet today."

"A diet?" He took a bite of eggs and dabbed his chin with his napkin. Donna nibbled her toast.

"Yeah," she said. "I want to lose a few pounds."

"I think you look great, honey."

"But *I* don't." She took another bite of toast. They finished breakfast in silence. When he was done, Donovan took his plate to the sink, poured himself a second cup of coffee, and went for the newspaper. He checked his watch again. It was 7:22.

When he returned to the kitchen, he kissed Donna once more. She blushed. "What was that for?"

"Nothing," he said. "I can just tell today's going to be a good day."

"Yeah?"

He nodded. "It's just a feeling, I guess. Besides, everything's still on schedule, so that always makes for a good day."

Donna chuckled. He delighted in her laughter. The sound of it made his heart skip a beat, and always brought a smile to his face. A good morning indeed. Still grinning, Donovan sat and unfolded his newspaper. There wasn't much worth reading—mostly articles about local politics, the announcement of a new reality television show's premiere, rising taxes, falling stocks, and so on. He beamed when he saw a familiar advertisement:

Has your identity been compromised? We can help! Contact Identinel, your security sentinel.

He'd worked for the company going on nine years, although it had been a bumpy road at first. Fresh out of college, he'd quickly learned that an English degree was useless. The liberal arts were sinking fast, and needing something to make ends meet, Donovan had finally taken a low-end position in the sales department of Identinel. Nine years later, he'd managed to work his way up the corporate ladder rung by agonizing rung, and now he was a team leader in his department. Sometime soon, hopefully tomorrow, he would receive another promotion. Spotting their latest ad in the paper was a good omen. He skimmed the rest of the paper and finished off his coffee.

"Anything good?"

He passed the newspaper down to her and shook his head.

"Same ol', same ol'."

The microwave clock read 7:39, which Donovan confirmed with his watch. If he left now, he'd make it to the office with a good twenty minutes or so to spare. His punctuality could earn him a few points when it came time for his review.

"I think I'm going to leave early today, hon."

"What's the rush?"

"No rush," he said, rising from the table. He took his jacket from the back of the chair and put it on. "That review's tomorrow. I want to impress Butler."

She snorted. "I hope he paid attention this time."

Donovan shared his wife's disdain. Impressing Butler was no easy task, given his inflated sense of self-accomplishment, but

Donovan had proven himself reliable and earned the highest sales record for four years in a row. How could he *not* have earned this promotion?

"I'd better be going," he said.

"Don't forget to charge the cell phone."

He double-checked his pocket, nodding as the phone knocked against his car keys. Donovan had resisted acquiring one for as long as he could, but Donna wore down his arguments, and they'd settled on a pre-paid model. A new addition to his morning routine, he struggled to remember it needed charging. The damn thing drained its battery almost every day.

"Got it."

Donna's attention remained with the newspaper. "Have a good day, dear."

"What, no kiss?"

She looked up at him, arching an eyebrow.

"You'll get more than that tonight, Donnie."

Donovan grinned, leaning over to kiss her. He felt a flush of heat in his cheeks. He loved it when she called him Donnie.

"Hold that thought," he told her, and opened the door. Their brown-haired Persian, Mr. Precious Paws, scampered out past him, furry head and tail held high. *Excuse me, your highness*, Donovan thought, winking at Donna before closing the door behind him.

He stood on the porch for the moment and breathed in the crisp, morning air. That phantom hand tugged at his gut for only a moment and then it was gone. Donovan steadied himself. He looked up. The sky was clear. Birds chirped overhead.

He slowly exhaled, and smiled.

A good day, he thought. *A very, very good day.*

•

The morning commute was bumper to bumper for most of the way, as it seemed to be on every weekday, but nothing could dampen his spirits. He began the day feeling that all would be well, and he wasn't about to give it up for a few angry drivers. The heavy traffic let up after ten minutes, and soon Donovan was speeding down the freeway listening to a morning radio host welcome a guest on the air.

He didn't pay much attention to their conversation—he was busy concentrating on the road and its collection of Monday morning idiots. Still, bits and pieces of the show worked their way into his thoughts. The guest was an author promoting his latest book.

"—itle of the book is *A Life Ordinary: A Comprehensive Study in Human Mediocrity.*"

Donovan frowned. A life ordinary? What was wrong with being ordinary? He was content with his life. Sure, he didn't have the best job in the world—not the kind he'd imagined having during those dreamy days of college—but for now he had to give up that youthful idealism and work nine-to-five like every other John. Q. Taxpayer.

Though Donovan still dreamed of writing the Great American Novel, the demands of work and marriage limited him to only an hour of writing per night. Perhaps, someday, it would be Donovan on the radio promoting his latest work. Floating in the back of Donovan's mind was an image: Seated in his home office, fingers poised over a computer keyboard, he could hear the echoes of his wife playing games with their children.

That fantasy took him away from the radio program and back to Donna's pleasant face. The two of them had wanted a baby for so long, and now, after several years of saving and planning, they were finally giving things a try. Every Monday, Wednesday, and Friday evening, Donovan and Donna made love with hope of conceiving a child. Sometimes he daydreamed about that happy day when he'd burst into the Identinel offices and proclaim "It's a boy!" Or a girl. He wasn't picky.

The radio program cut to a commercial as Donovan took his exit. He looked at the console clock: 8:38. The lights at each intersection turned green upon his approach, and he sped through them without interruption. When he reached the Identinel parking lot, he pulled into a space near those reserved for upper management.

The odd pulling sensation in his stomach intensified as he walked across the lot toward the building. He paused at the door, took a breath, and put his hand on his belly. *What did I eat last night?*

His stomach lurched, accenting his recollection of the mystery meal: curry. He'd had curry the night before.

Donovan shook off the discomfort, promising himself antacids for lunch, and pushed his way into the building.

•

Click.

Donovan removed his headset and sighed. Another sale lost. He tapped a few keys on the keyboard, adding another phone number to the growing "no call" list. The old tricks to save that sale just weren't working anymore, and people did not want to guard their identities as much as they should.

From somewhere beyond his cubicle, he heard the screeching call of the Two Tammys, Identinel's dual Human Resources Coordinators. Tammy Perpa and Tammy Quilago formed an unholy union of professionalism, leaving most employees trembling in their wake. The mere sounds of their voices stirred the acid in his stomach, the effect making him nauseous.

Around the office, many called them "The Terrible Tammys." Tomorrow, along with Butler, they would preside over Donovan's review. Understandably, this did little to ease the tightening discomfort in his gut. It slowly climbed up into his chest, giving pause to his heart for a brief moment, and he had to gasp for breath. Then, as quickly as it came, the phantom grip around his torso was gone.

He stood, peeked over the wall of his cube, and watched the two women make their way down the main aisle of the call center. After an unproductive morning, the last thing he wanted was a conversation with them about performance.

Donovan ducked back into his cube to check the time again: 10:30. He reached for his coffee cup—a custom-made mug featuring a screen print of Mr. Precious Paws—and made his way to the employee lounge. The Terrible Tammys were no longer in sight.

The lounge was furnished with two refrigerators, three microwaves, and four coffeepots. A lonely water cooler sat in a corner. A few of Donovan's coworkers loitered around the tables in the room, chatting about their weekend exploits. Donovan, on the other hand, wasn't there to make small talk. He needed coffee.

"Hey, Candle!"

Timothy Butler entered the room with a grin that cut across his face. The other employees scattered. Donovan shot a quick glance over his shoulder, muttered "Shit" under his breath, and began to pour his coffee.

Just smile, he told himself. It wasn't that simple. When Donovan did not respond, Butler repeated himself. Donovan closed his eyes for a moment. His name was *Donovan* Candle. Not just "Candle." Butler's insistence on dropping a person's first name was grating on even the best of days. Donovan tried to maintain his composure.

"Morning," he said. He poured cream and sugar into his coffee.

"How was your weekend, Candle? Mine was great—"

Oh really? How great was it?

Timothy Butler yammered on. For Donovan, knowing his boss spoke only to hear his own voice made his presence all the more intolerable.

The discomfort in his stomach returned with force, startling him so badly that he almost dropped his mug. A few drops of coffee spilled onto the counter. Butler's words—something about a weekend, a lake, time on a boat with his wife—ran together, and for a few agonizing seconds, all Donovan could hear was a low, metallic drone.

What the hell is happening to me?

The feeling ceased. Butler was still talking. Donovan put a hand to his forehead, and it came away slick with sweat.

"—played eighteen holes after we got home from the beach on Sund—"

Donovan knew this conversation, had heard it a thousand times before. He'd seen others caught in this same corner, forced to listen to Butler's monologue about weekend excursions, and now it was his turn again. After nine years Donovan had learned to tune him out.

He stirred his coffee. The sensation swelled in the pit of his stomach once more, but only for an instant. *Maybe Butler's sucking the life out of me*, he mused. The thought made him smile.

"So, yeah, how was your weekend, Candle?" Butler clapped a hand on Donovan's back, causing him to spill a few more drops of coffee, this time onto his shoes. He looked into his boss' cold, blue eyes and forced a smile.

"It was a weekend."

Staring into his superior's face, Donovan was reminded of how little he'd accomplished—how, after nine years, he'd advanced only one or two rungs up the corporate ladder. Timothy Butler, only a few years older, had a much higher salary and a more fulfilling life. Would these things be Donovan's in the years to come?

Yes, he told himself. He wanted the extravagant stories and financial freedom. He wanted that new TV, he wanted to buy Donna that jewelry she'd had her eye on, he wanted to finish that novel. He wanted to remodel the guest room, to have a child, to build a legacy and pass it on.

He wanted life with all its trimmings. Staring into Butler's eyes, he realized he'd have to work harder, to toil and reach for that goal. He'd have to want it more than anything else.

"Mr. Butler," he heard himself say. Butler's eyes seemed to reflect the sparkle of his perfect teeth.

"What's up, Candle?"

"Just wanted to remind you about my review tomorrow."

Butler's expression faded, and for a moment Donovan feared the man had forgotten about his review, but then his face lit up and he said, "Don't worry, amigo! It's all taken care of!"

Relief came over him, but it was short-lived. As Timothy Butler walked away, Donovan saw the man's reassuring facade fall away for an instant. He stood there, not quite sure whether it was his imagination or something more sinister. Butler's expression seemed so conniving. It made him uneasy, a feeling that followed him back to his desk.

There he finished his coffee and continued working through his lunch hour, making cold calls to customers in an attempt to sell them a service they did not want. As the hours crawled by, he found he was unable to escape the black cloud of Butler's mysterious expression. All afternoon, he struggled to determine just what it was that worried him.

Was it that he did not trust his own boss? Was it the insincerity in Butler's eyes that put him on edge? He thought about asking around the office, but that would only lead to gossip, and this would be better played close to the chest. Even so, uncertainty nagged him. It encompassed his mind so completely, that he almost missed the clock striking 5:00 P.M. The entire day was lost to an odd hint of suspicion.

He felt like a failure when he left the office. His sales for the day were the lowest in months. People under his wing—even new hires still in training—had made more sales that day. Donovan had no one to blame but himself. He wanted to blame Timothy Butler, but his rational self spoke too loudly to be ignored. *It's all you*, it told him. *Quit worrying and get on with it.*

Donovan sat in his car for a few minutes, waiting for the emptiness to subside. When it did, he felt the first pangs of hunger rumbling in his stomach, accenting that deeper, more troubling sensation. He tried to ignore it.

Traffic was less agreeable that evening. Shortly after taking the highway entrance ramp, Donovan found himself sitting bumper-to-bumper with other lost souls trying to get home. He switched on the radio to help pass the time. A recap of the morning's interview was playing, and this time Donovan caught the name of the book's author.

"Please welcome Dr. Albert Sparrow—"

Outside, an SUV blared its horn and sped around Donovan's car. He gripped the steering wheel and tried to focus on the road.

"Thank you," said Dr. Sparrow.

"I understand you've got a new book available?"

"Yes, the title is—"

Donovan chimed in, "*A Life Ordinary: A Comprehensive Study in Human Mediocrity.*" He snorted at the sound of it. *So pretentious.*

"Care to give us the gist, Doc?"

"Through my studies, I've found that most people live painfully boring lives. We get up, we go to work, we slave away for eight, ten, even twelve hours a day, only to go home and meander for a few more before sleep."

"Yep," the host chortled. "Sounds about right."

"Over the last five years I've studied this phenomenal tendency toward the ordinary life. While some of my contemporaries refute my argument, I believe atypical activity is essential for our species to survive."

"So, what, we should go camping or something every other weekend?"

"Not exactly, for even in such an escape we may confine ourselves to routine. Our failure to recognize these patterns leads to a kind of ennui which—"

"On-what?"

"Ennui. It's—"

Donovan changed the station. Dr. Albert Sparrow was replaced by the screeching singer of AC/DC. He'd rather listen to this than the boorish ramblings of an overpaid PhD. He tuned out a second helping of the aging rockers. The music was interrupted by a Missing Persons alert for someone named Alice Walenta.

As he listened, that faint, metallic buzzing filled his ears. He grimaced at the sound and switched off the radio to help clear his head. The droning stopped. By the time he pulled into his driveway, he'd forgotten all about the good Dr. Sparrow, AC/DC, and Timothy Butler. For a day begun with such high hopes, it had fallen far below the mark.

For now, Donovan was just happy to be home.

•

Donna dabbed the corners of her mouth with a napkin. Steam from a platter of broiled chicken rose between them.

"Uh huh?" he mumbled between bites.

"I was wondering if we could, you know, maybe take a vacation?"

"A vacation?"

"Not for a week or anything. Just, I don't know, a long weekend?"

He swallowed his chicken, cut another piece, and asked, "When? To where?"

"I don't know, Don. I thought we could go to the shore. It would be nice."

Donovan finished his chicken, washed it down with a glass of iced tea, and released a low belch. He excused himself, then stood and walked to the fridge to examine their cat-themed calendar. A kitten-shaped magnet held it to the refrigerator door.

"We could go early next month," she offered, "before the tourists start to arrive."

He flipped back and forth between the current month and the next, frowning. "Honey, I—" he began, but then interrupted himself. "Oh hell."

"What?"

He held out the calendar page and pointed to a circled date. "Today's the 16th."

Donna shrugged. "So?"

"It's Michael's birthday."

Before she could say anything else, he reaffixed the calendar to the fridge door and reached for the wall-mounted phone. He lifted the receiver from its cradle and dialed. Donna sighed and mumbled something. He turned away just as she rose from her seat to begin clearing the table. By the time his brother answered the phone, she was already running water in the sink.

"Hello?"

Donna clanged dishes into the sink basin.

"Mike," Donovan said. "Happy birthday."

Michael Candle chuckled. "Oh. Damn, already?"

"Wasn't sure I'd catch you at home. Figured you'd be out chasing crooks and the like."

"Ah well, you know me. Always busy."

Although Donovan grew up reading the work of Raymond Chandler, he never fashioned himself as much of a detective. His brother, on the other hand, eschewed the fiction of their youth and chose to make detective work his career. Donovan admired Michael's dedication to hard-boiled facts, so it didn't surprise him when Michael struck out on his own as a licensed private investigator.

Whenever Donovan spoke about his brother, he was always sure to mention Michael's career as a Private Eye.

Donna turned off the faucet. Dishes clanked together in the sink.

"So . . ." his brother said. The lingering tension in his voice made Donovan uncomfortable. "What's up, Don? How's life?"

He sucked in his breath. He pictured his brother on the other end of the line, his arms crossed, with a contrived smirk on his face. Their conversations, however innocent, always shifted focus to Donovan's quality of life. It could only get worse. He cleared his throat and tried to redirect the conversation's flow.

"Same as usual. Say, have you spoken to the folks lately?"

"Nah. You?"

"A couple weeks ago. They called from Rio."

"Rio de Janeiro?"

"Yeah. Crazy, isn't it?"

Their parents always spoke of seeing the world after they retired. Now, with their father's pension paid out, they decided to make good on their dream. Their travel agent booked a month-long continent hop. Imagining his folks reclining on some white-sanded beach along the Equator made him smile. He glanced over at Donna. He hoped they would be able to travel someday.

His face fell when he remembered her request for a weekend vacation. Maybe they could, but not in the near future. They had to save their money for the baby.

"Don? You there?"

"Huh? Yeah. Sorry, just spaced out for a sec."

"I asked how the wife's doing?"

He looked at Donna. He could see the rigid frown on her face as she finished the dishes.

"Donna's just fine. Feisty as ever."

She paused for a moment, shot him a quick glance, then splashed her hands back into the dishwater.

"How's—how's *your* girl? Jennifer, right? Any kids yet?"

It was laughable, the thought of Michael having children. He was too wrapped up in his own life to focus on kids. It was astounding that he even had time to date. Donovan hadn't met Michael's new girlfriend, but he hoped to soon. From what his brother told him, she seemed lovely, a perfect match.

Michael said, "No, no kids yet."

"You know, Donna and I are trying. You might be an u—"

"You still a phone jockey?"

Donovan closed his mouth. *Uncle*, he finished. Thick pockets of heat collected around his face, accenting his shame. The phone's plastic casing popped, and he realized he was gripping it too hard. That invisible hand began to pull at his midsection again, working its nonexistent fingers around his spine and threatening to pluck him away. Donovan heard a hiss of static, and then it was gone.

He collected himself, measured his words. They came slowly.

"Yes. I still for work Identinel."

Michael chuckled. Donovan imagined his brother's smug grin. It was an expression he knew well. While growing up, his brother picked on him for burying himself in his books, mocking his choice to view life through imaginary eyes rather than living in reality. Even now, at the age of thirty-two, Michael's condescension still pulled at Donovan's strings. Michael knew this, and that made it even worse.

"You need to live a little, Don."

"I'm happy with the way things are, Mike."

It was the same conversation as always. Why did it always come to this?

"No, Donovan," his brother said, "I don't think you are. I really don't. And you want to know why?"

I'm sure you'll tell me anyway, Donovan thought, biting his lip in silence.

"It's because you have no life. Not really. You only think you're happy because that phone jockey job—"

"I'm one of the top salesmen—"

"—Whatever. That job is all you know. You've worked there, what, ten years? Twelve?"

"Nine," Donovan muttered. The phone's casing popped again. He relaxed his fingers.

"Nine years and you're a top salesman. I thought you wanted to write, Don. What happened to that book you were working on?"

He sighed. *Every damn time.* It always turned into a bickering contest, revolving around how his older brother thought he should live his life. There was always that air of elitism hanging over every conversation, about how Donovan wasn't living up to his expectations, how he was letting himself and his wife down by not reaching his potential.

Donovan frowned. *Somehow*, he thought, *Michael's always been happier. Always more successful.* It was true. Once Michael knew what he wanted, he went after it, not stopping until it was his. Donovan, on the other hand, meandered. He wasn't sure what he wanted. As the years slipped by, he chose the path of least resistance, and now he was frowned upon for swimming with the current. Perhaps that was what he didn't understand: how someone who went against the grain could be so successful, while he—the more compliant of the two—remained static.

"Go out, Don. Take Donna and just go somewhere. Do something, don't just plan it. Pick up your shit and go, man. Otherwise you're just living in a box while the world moves on without you."

"I can't afford to," he snapped. His voice was shaky, eyes watering, and a lump had lodged itself in his throat. Worse, the weird indigestion kept coming back. Sweat dotted his forehead. In the span of the last five minutes he was reduced to a bullied six year-old all over again.

"And that's because—"

"Look," he said, "I'm sorry I didn't live up to your expectations. I'm sorry I don't live the glamorous lifestyle, Mr. Private *Dick*. My job is my job and it pays my bills."

"It pays your bills," Michael countered, "and that's all. To top it off, your job is sucking the life out of you one day at a time."

"No." It was a weak reply. He slammed one hand against the refrigerator door. It startled Donna, and she dropped a plate into the sink. "It's just a job. I'm still working on that novel. One day soon—"

Michael sighed. "Y'know what I want for my birthday, little brother?"

"What?"

"For you to get a fucking life."

He scrambled for a retort, could even feel it climbing up the back of his throat, warm and boiling with venom—

But the line was dead. The dial tone hummed in his ear. He hung up the phone and turned. Donna leaned against the counter with her arms folded across her chest and a damp dish towel hanging over shoulder.

"How's your brother?"

Donovan stared at her, noting the slant of her lips and the glint in her eyes. He knew that look. He knew he should choose his words carefully, with little hesitation.

"He's an asshole."

"What did he say?"

"Same old crap about how I should find another job, how I'm not really living, blah, blah, blah."

He twirled one finger in the air. Mr. Precious Paws pranced into the room and rubbed against his leg. He knelt, picked up the cat, and scratched between his ears.

Donna frowned. She turned back to the sink, reached into its murky water, and pulled the plug.

Donovan said nothing. He kept scratching the cat between his ears. The dishwater gurgled as it went down the drain, and he cleared his throat when it finished.

"So, about that vacation."

"Just forget I said anything, Don."

There it was. The tone. It grated down his spine.

"Honey, you know we can't—"

"And why not?" She tossed the dish towel onto the counter.

"We can't afford it."

"We *can* afford it." She turned to face him. "I'm not sure what your brother said to you, but I've got a pretty good idea."

She counted off details of their conversation with her fingers. "He probably asked you about your job. He asked how long you've worked there—"

He smirked. "You're pretty good at this."

"—and how you've not done anything with your life because you don't have one. Am I right? Am I in the ballpark, Donovan?"

His face fell. His mouth was dry. Donna shook her head.

"If you don't want to go, just tell me. Don't give me the same excuse as everything else. We can afford it, Don. I can check the savings account too, you know."

He chewed his lower lip. "But we have to save for the baby, Donna."

"I just—" She stammered. "I just want to do something with

our lives, Don. It's always save, save, save, and for what?" She paused, held back a sob, and said, "It's not about the money. You know that. We don't have to stay at a five-star resort. I would be happy just driving to the shore for a day, but you won't let me finish. You've already made up your mind."

The first tears streamed down her cheeks.

"Face it," she went on, "your brother's right. You live for that job, and nothing else. Money, time, routine—it's all that's important to you, and what you earn is never enough for you."

He squeezed Mr. Precious Paws tightly enough to elicit a low growl from the feline.

"That's not true."

Donna wiped the tears from her face. "Then take a day off."

"To do what?"

"Nothing!" she shouted. "Absolutely nothing! Not a goddamn thing!"

"But—"

"But what?"

He searched for an answer. A plausible answer. One that would make sense to her in this state. He scratched away at the interior of his own mind looking for the perfect thing to say, and still he came up with the very excuse he'd tried to avoid.

"But we have to save."

Donna forced a smile, shook her head, and made her way out of the room. A few moments later the back patio door opened and closed. His words hung in the air, thickening, weighing down upon him.

He *had* a life, damnit. He had a wife, a job, a house, maybe a child—what more to life could there be? Had he missed some vital detail about growing up—something explaining the details of having a "life?"

Mr. Precious Paws yowled and scratched at his cheek. He flinched, yelped in pain, and watched as the feline ran for the stairs. He realized he'd squeezed the cat too hard, a victim of his tense reverie. He stood there for only a moment longer, rubbing the scratch and nursing a battered ego. He looked at his watch: 6:49. Within the span of twenty minutes, he'd managed to alienate every member of his family. That was a personal record.

•

Donovan retreated to his office. It was at times like this that he tried to escape into the world of his novel in an attempt to pull out something good and productive. His characters—the disillusioned Joe Hopper, a hard-boiled Private Eye, and the often philosophical, often dangerous Mistress Colby—were experiencing their plight as two human beings trying to survive in the decline of Western culture. Donovan pecked at the keyboard for an hour, listening to the crooning, Southern drawl of Hopper in his own head. When he typed a thousand words, he stopped to read over them.

Ain't no good, boss, Hopper said. Donovan frowned and deleted them all. He started again.

It had been like this for over a year. Every evening he would sit down to work out the details of the plot's climax, and no matter how much he wrote, no matter the quality, it would always end in deletion. The story was frozen on page 299.

After a second attempt and another deleted set of words, he sat back in his chair and shook his head. The cursor blinked.

He leaned forward, buried his head in his hands, and muttered, "I don't know anymore."

Tonight just wasn't his night. The day was shot, and the evening wasn't shaping up to be much better.

He looked back at the stack of pages on his desk. The first 299 pages of his magnum opus stared back. No matter how hard he tried to get into the groove of writing, he could not. His head was clouded by conversations with his brother and his wife. Memories of Timothy Butler's contrived grin only served to drive the feeling home. And there was that damn indigestion, too.

Perhaps Identinel *was* sucking the life from him. He had to consider the possibility. Had he made the right choice by staying with the company for so long, rather than working for a few years before moving on to greener pastures? *Of course*, he told himself. *I've made enough money to sustain the both of us for years.*

Donna's voice chimed in his head, *It's not about the money.*

And it wasn't. He knew that. Turning in his seat, Donovan stared at the document on his screen. He frowned. *Should've finished this damn thing by now*, he thought. *I could've pumped out five novels in the time I've spent on this one.*

He thought about Joe Hopper, and wished life could truly imitate art. He wished he had the guts to face an uncertain future, walk into work tomorrow, and tell Butler to cram the review up his ass. It was something Hopper would do with Southern grace and style. It was something Michael Candle might do, too.

Staring at the great white nothing beneath page 299, Donovan suddenly saw the story's faults. Page 300 would never be realized, because nothing had really happened in the previous 299. He'd fallen into complacency with the story, certain that this was the best it could be. In that security, he'd resigned his characters to the same fate.

He'd lost his drive, his vision. To fix the story, he realized, he would have to start over. He closed the document and deleted the file. The indigestion, which had grown from an occasional discomfort to a constant, annoying sensation, relented for a brief moment.

Maybe I'm getting an ulcer.

He looked at the blank page and was just about to type "The Great American Novel by Donovan Candle" when he glanced at the clock. He smiled, closed the document, and turned off the computer. It was three minutes to nine o'clock.

"Almost forgot," he said to the empty room, "it's time for *CSI*."

•

The discomfort in his stomach grew worse as the minutes passed. It wasn't pain, so much as uneasiness building up within him. A few times, a sharp droning chime filled his head, making it hard to concentrate on the screen.

Donovan tiptoed into the bedroom half an hour after Donna retired. He thought about waking her to tell her about the strange sensation he felt, but that would make him even more of a jerk. Whatever it was, it didn't hurt, and so he decided to take it like a man.

Donna stirred as he crawled into bed. She rolled to her side, facing him. He pulled the blanket over himself and stared at the ceiling.

Her fingertips brushed his arm, and when he looked over he saw that her eyes were open.

"Hi," he said. She smiled, leaned forward, and kissed him. That kiss led to another. He began to say something, but she pressed her finger against his lips. She sat up and climbed on top of him. He gasped when she took him in her hand and slid him into her.

They made love for what seemed like an hour, their bodies entwined in a chaos of sheets and blankets, until they collapsed into one another with one, climactic shiver. Sweaty, dizzy, Donovan leaned back against the headboard and sighed. He closed his eyes. Donna raised up, kissed his forehead, and said, "I love you, Donnie."

"I love you too," he said, opening his eyes and expecting to see her there. Only she wasn't. She'd rolled away from him.

"I'm still mad at you, though," she said. He remained there for a moment longer before uttering a long, low sigh. The room suddenly felt cold, gray. The weird pull in his gut strengthened. He closed his eyes and rolled over, trying his best to ignore the feeling. For now, Donovan was just happy to go to sleep.

•

His night was filled with odd, troubling dreams. The alarm woke him, and he silenced its blaring beep on his way to the bathroom.

He yawned, fumbling for the light switch along the wall. Barely able to make out shapes in the dark, Donovan didn't trust himself to piss without a light. His fingers found the switch; light filled the room.

Donovan dismissed what he saw as a figment of his lingering dream state, as though somehow his brain wasn't quite tuned in and was sending static to his senses. *Wake up*, he told himself. *Early bird and all that crap.*

He rubbed his eyes, blinked, even splashed his face with water in an attempt to uncross the wires in his brain, but it was still happening. The pull in his stomach was now greater than ever. The phantom hand yanked at his guts, threatening to pull him right out of reality. He almost didn't mind it, would've *preferred* it to what he saw happening before his eyes.

He held out his hand, staring in slack-jawed terror as his skin—flesh, meat, bone, *all* of him—flickered in and out of existence. For a split-second, Donovan Candle seemed to disappear, and the only thing that kept him rooted in that waking reality was the sound of his horrified scream.

-2-
THE FLICKERING

He silenced himself, watching his reflection flicker, fade, and return to full opacity. He stared at one hand, then the other. Was he dreaming? He had to be. Things like this did not happen. He ran cold water over his hands, half expecting it to pass through his palms, but instead it pooled and spilled over into the sink. Now, certain that he was truly awake, he stared at his hands once more. They were solid, just as they should be.

Get a grip, boss. It was too early for Hopper's quips. Donovan pushed the thought aside, leaned forward, and took a long look at his reflection.

"Just a dream," he muttered to himself. "Sleep walking. That's all."

The uncomfortable force wrenched at his gut so hard that he doubled over the sink. He fought off nausea and the surging drone in his head. *Keep it together*, he thought. *Just getting sick, is all. Take a shower.*

The warm water delivered him from the sickening feeling, and he let his mind wander. Perhaps he was sleepwalking? He'd read about it happening to people of all ages. It was a sound conclusion, one that put him at ease. He chuckled about it, his voice a hollow echo in the shower stall. *What a strange dream*, he thought. *Almost like I wasn't there—like a projection.*

He burst into laughter and reached down to turn off the water. His hands faded in unison, followed by his arms. His laughter twisted into a shriek. He ran his hands over himself, down his torso, hips, manhood, and buttocks. All of him seemed to fade in and out like static, his skin first growing transparent, then vanishing entirely for an instant before reappearing as solid matter.

Donovan pushed open the shower door and returned to the mirror, staring in abject horror as his own reflection dimmed and faded.

"Donna," he muttered. It was low at first, then grew to a trembling plea. "*Donna!*"

He staggered down the hall, leaving a trail of damp carpet in his wake. The alarm clock on the nightstand read 6:40—just five minutes shy of Donna's alarm.

"Honey."

She stirred beneath the blankets. Frightened, Donovan's eyes darted between his fading self and his sleeping wife. Beads of water rolled down his forehead and fell to the floor.

"Donna?" He nudged one of her exposed feet.

She grunted. "What, Don?"

"Honey, there's something wrong. I—"

Donna sat up, squinting at him. "Where're your clothes?"

Her question seemed strange to him. What did it matter where his clothes were? He stared at her, held out his fading, flickering hands, and frowned. Water dripped onto the bed.

"I was in the shower, and—"

"And you're still wet. You're dripping all over the floor, Don. Go get a towel. Jeez."

Donna pulled back the blankets and gasped when her feet met damp carpet. She glared at him. He stood there, naked and soaked, with both hands held out in a gesture of confused apology. His stomach lurched again as his skin flickered into a transparent state.

"Don't you see this?"

She looked at him, groggy-eyed and puzzled. "See what?"

"*This!*" He held out his arms. The pull in his abdomen settled down. His skin returned to normal, as if to mock him.

Donna covered a yawn. He watched her in disbelief. How could she not see? Was this some sort of weird head game, a throwback to their previous evening's argument? No, he realized, that couldn't be it. They'd known each other for too long to sink to such petty levels. Besides, he knew she loved him too much to ignore something as serious as this.

"I *see* you making a mess I'll have to clean up. And," she fought back another yawn, "I *see* that if I don't get some coffee soon, I'm going to bite off your head."

Donna pushed past him, uttered a small sigh when she saw the soaked trail to the bathroom, and went downstairs to the kitchen. Donovan stared at his hands again and flinched as his flesh began to deteriorate once more.

I have to be dreaming, he thought. *I have to be—*

The second alarm startled him. He reached over, turned it off, and fanned out his fingers. They were there, and yet they weren't, fading from opaque to translucent, from flesh to nothing and back again.

You ain't dreamin, boss. Hopper again. He cursed his imagination for breeding a Southern detective, and cursed himself for letting the character become the voice of his inner monologue.

More water dripped from his arm. He regarded his hands once more with caution before retreating to the bathroom for a towel.

•

After a couple of ill-fated attempts, he decided to skip shaving. His flesh vanished every time he began to drag the blade across his face. The last thing he wanted was to misjudge and leave a large, unshaven patch of hair across his chin—or worse, to slit his own throat. Getting dressed was just as difficult. His leg would waver, dim, and vanish each time he tried to put on his trousers. Once clothed, he found his shirt and pants flickered along with the rest of him.

When he finally made it downstairs, Donna watched him with mild irritation. An empty bowl sat before his place at the table along with a box of cereal. On most mornings he ventured downstairs to find a hot breakfast waiting for him. Today he took the hint. She was still angry, but for God's sake, couldn't she see what was happening to him?

Donovan ate his cereal in silence. Mr. Precious Paws traveled into the kitchen and sat at his feet. The cat looked up at him with wide eyes, ears perked with attentive curiosity. When Donovan lifted a spoonful, his hand dimmed and flashed out of reality. A quick jerk in his gut startled him. He dropped the spoon, startling Mr. Precious Paws out of his reverent stare, and frowned as the cat scampered away.

For a moment the room went gray, and the pull in his stomach exerted such force that he cried out in pain. He blinked tears from his eyes and stared about the room. Its warmth was gone, replaced with a stagnant, cold grayish tone that seemed to cover every surface. Donna was cast in its hue as she poured herself a bowl of cereal.

He blinked. Color returned to the room.

"Donna," he whispered, "there is something wrong."

She flipped through the morning newspaper, seemingly oblivious to his statement. He reached down, picked up his spoon, then leaned forward to stare at his wife.

"Donna."

Nothing. Not so much as a raised eyebrow.

Mr. Precious Paws wandered over, stood on his hind legs, and scratched at Donovan's knee. He yelped, startled by the prickle of the cat's claws, and kicked his leg. The cat yowled and slid across the kitchen floor, colliding against the cabinetry with a soft thump.

"Don't kick the cat."

He looked back at his wife. She glared at him, her lips pulled into a frown. He held up his trembling hands and twiddled his fingers.

"Look at this," he said flatly. All ten digits vacillated between solidity and transparency.

She strained to look at him. After a moment of eye contact, Donna put a hand to her temple and began to rub.

"What?"

"This," he said, and recoiled as his hands flashed in and out of existence. He'd been faced with the sight for almost half an hour now, but it was something he doubted he'd ever get used to. How could he? To see one's own self fading away like a ghost was unnerving, unsettling—it only happened in the movies, not in reality, yet even on film it carried an element of startling horror.

"Sorry." She rubbed at her temple and went back to the newspaper. "I have a headache, and you aren't helping."

His heart dropped into his stomach. *She can't see*, he realized. He placed both hands on his knees and frowned. Had he finally snapped? Was this hallucinatory transparency just the first step? He wondered if other strange mental anomalies would follow—strange, impossible delusions like flying elephants or a perceived ability to walk through walls.

He tried to work out what was happening to him, but all he could do was stare at his skin, at the way it faded and filled with a flesh-colored static. His vision danced from a full spectrum of color to cold shades of gray. This effect lasted only for a fraction of a second, but was obvious enough for him to notice. Color-blindness along with insanity? He grew so distracted by these disturbing possibilities that time slipped by him. Donna snapped him out of these troubled musings.

"Don," she said, "you're going to be late."

"Late?" He scrambled to his feet. "What time—"

His eyes fell upon the microwave clock. It read 8:05 in large, digital numbers.

"Oh hell."

Donovan quickly kissed his wife's cheek, grabbed his keys, and darted out the door.

•

Donna was puzzled by the exchange. She sat back in her seat and rubbed at her temples once more. It was an ungodly headache. It sliced through her thoughts with measured, low throbs.

Her husband's behavior meandered on the strange side of things. *It's just stress*, she told herself. *Just stress over his review—*

A drone of noise surged through her head, filling it with an interminable buzzing. She lost her concentration. For a moment she stared off into space, lost in a white, agonizing static. Finally, after a few seconds, the buzzing stopped. Donna looked about the room, then down at her feet. Mr. Precious Paws stared up at her.

"What's up, Paws?"

The cat blinked. Donna reached down and scratched between his ears.

"Good kitty."

She went back to her reading. The headache did not return.

•

Driving on Tuesdays was no different than on Mondays. The same traffic, the same commute, the same moronic drivers. The commute was the reason he left earlier than necessary every morning. Now he was one of those morons, leaving too late and driving too fast to make up for lost time. He honked the horn and screamed as another driver cut him off without so much as a turn signal.

"It's okay," he told himself. His voice was distant and empty in the absence of the usual radio banter, but he couldn't bear listening to morning radio personalities go on about inane garbage. His mind was elsewhere. "There's an explanation. Always an explanation."

His hands flickered, disappeared, and reappeared on the wheel. Though he still maintained the sensation of touch, he could not see his own flesh, and the very idea horrified him. He wondered if he should go see a doctor. *And just what the hell would you tell 'em, hoss?*

Donovan didn't have an answer to that. A red Suburban came to a stop ahead of him, and he slammed on the brakes just in time.

A logical explanation. There had to be one. He retraced his steps in hope that somewhere along the way his memory might creep upon an answer. Perhaps he'd inhaled a toxic fume of some kind, or maybe come into contact with a top secret skin agent that could render a person completely invisible. Those thoughts seemed so implausible, but they ran wild through his mind, by-products of a vivid imagination.

After sitting at a stand-still for a full ten minutes, Donovan came to a simple conclusion: he watched too much television.

People did not vanish—at least, not like this. His hands flickered again. He saw the steering wheel through them.

I'm crazy, he thought. *I am certifiable.*

The explanation did not sit well with him. It made his stomach lurch. The world went gray for a blink before shifting back to an otherwise colorful morning. The most damning piece of evidence to support his newfound insanity was Donna's inability to see the phenomenon. He considered the possibility that she was angry enough to ignore his malady, but even that did not make sense. *Pissed or not, she wouldn't do that to me.*

Traffic lurched forward once more. Donovan took his exit. The dashboard clock read 8:49. He tried to ignore it and pressed his foot on the gas.

"Come on," he said, smiling at the purr of the engine. He came off the exit ramp and sped through the intersection just as the traffic light turned red.

He was just two blocks from the office when he spotted red and blue flashing lights in the rearview mirror. As the police cruiser neared, he caught a glimpse of his own reflection. His face, eyes, forehead, thinning hairline—all disappeared before his eyes. The world went gray again, turning the cruiser's red and blues into meaningless shades.

"No," he moaned. "*No.*"

The officer flipped on the siren. Donovan frowned, signaled, and pulled the car into an empty gas station parking lot. The clock read 8:56. In four minutes, he would be late for the first time in nine years.

•

He shoved the ticket in his pocket and sat down at his desk. His watch read 9:22. He checked his phone and discovered three missed calls—one each from Tammy Quilago, Tammy Perpa, and Timothy Butler.

His legs turned to limp noodles, his arms and stomach to jelly, and he could feel his pulse on the back of his tongue. For the first time since waking, Donovan did not seem to mind that he was disappearing. In fact, at that moment, he wanted nothing more than to vanish from the face of the planet.

According to the messages, his superiors were waiting for him in the conference room. On any other day he could have shrugged off the meeting, walked into the conference room calm and collected. But today? Today he had a five o'clock shadow at nine in the morning, a $90 speeding ticket, and an order of invisibility with a side of colorblindness. His plate was full.

"Oh hell." He leaned over to pull up both pant legs. His left sock was blue; the right was brown. His hairy shins flickered as if to mock him.

A young woman walked past his cubicle just as he dimmed. She said nothing. He sighed, rose from his seat, and made his way down the aisle toward the conference room.

One of his coworkers, Phillip, got up from his seat as he passed.

"Good morning, Don."

"Morning, Phil."

The young man seemed to recoil at the sound of his voice. He pinched the space between his eyes. The room went gray, and Donovan thought he saw movement over Phil's shoulder. He blinked. Everything was back to normal—except for Phil. He was very pale.

"You all right?"

Phil said nothing. He pushed past Donovan and hurried to the restroom.

Work carried on around him, and no one else seemed to notice his strange affliction. Their attentions were focused on their monitors while they spoke into headsets, performing monotone sales pitches about a full range of Identinel's services. He passed a trainee on her way to the employee lounge and felt himself flicker as he opened his mouth to say hello. She simply smiled and went on her way.

A gut-wrenching thought occurred to him: his symptoms really were figments of his imagination. It explained everything, including Donna's apathy. *I've lost my mind*, he thought. He reconsidered going to see a doctor, particularly one of the psychiatric variety. *You best stop that*, Hopper scolded. *You got other things to be done 'sides bellyachin'.*

Donovan obeyed his creation and made his way to the conference room. He stood outside for a moment, sucked in his breath, and waited for his pounding heart to calm itself. When he was finished, he entered the room.

•

The conference room was sterile. Its white walls were accented by a pair of large, potted plants which sat in opposite corners at the far end. In the center was a long table, around which sat Timothy Butler, Tammy Quilago, and Tammy Perpa.

He stood, hands clasped behind his back, and tried to smile while the icy fingers of the phantom hand yanked at his insides. His smile came as a strained gesture as he tried to conceal his discomfort. They paid him a series of short glances before returning their attention to the pages of Donovan's file. The Tammys put their hands to their heads almost in unison, squinting as they tried to read the words on the page. Butler dug a finger into his ear.

Can they even see me? he wondered. His fear grew with each passing second. Finally, after a full minute of waiting, Butler spoke.

"Have a seat, Don." Butler motioned to the table.

He sat. Tammy Quilago shot him a cold smile before looking away. He realized none of them would make eye contact.

"Let's get started, shall we?"

Donovan nodded. He wipe his sweaty palms on his trousers. Yesterday, he was prepared for this. He knew what he would say in response to their questions. Today he found the words weren't there. They were stolen from him by an apparent lapse of sanity.

"Mr. Candle," Tammy Quilago said, "we commend you for nine whole years of service."

Tammy P. chirped, "That's quite a feat!"

"Indeed." Tammy Q. nodded. "Turn-over rates in this business are embarrassingly high. It's employees like yourself that keep Identinel ahead of the game."

She looked down at a sheet of paper. Her script. Donovan wondered how many other employees had heard this spiel. She began to speak again, but he could not hear her. A series of chimes rose in his ears, filling his head with the drone of distant bells, signaling his further descent into madness. His skin prickled, blinked out, and reappeared. He held his breath, expecting one of them to say something, but he was met with a silence that confirmed his suspicions. He was on his own.

The chimes slowed just as Tammy Q. finished her part of the script. It was Tammy P.'s turn to go over the review's structure. When she was done, Butler cleared his throat and flashed Donovan that award-winning smile. Sweat beaded on his forehead.

"Got any questions for us so far, Candle?"

"No."

"Good," he said. "First off, let's discuss your punctuality."

Donovan slumped back in his seat. He put a hand to his forehead. That prickly feeling crept up again. It felt as if thousands of insects crawled across his skin. Butler spoke, but Donovan could not understand him. He tried focusing on the man's words, but the more he tried, the more incomprehensible they became.

His vision went gray again. It lingered this time, and he watched in panic as objects lost their color. His coworkers became silhouettes. The walls and furniture lost their texture, appearing as simple, geometric shapes. The air had no warmth, and it was possessed of an unsettling gravity that pulled against him. He felt its familiar grip down in the center of his gut.

What the hell is happening to me? Even Joe Hopper was silent in his mind. There were no answers for this. He wanted to flee the room, race back to his car, and check himself into a mental hospital before something worse happened. Instead he remained frozen in place, unable to make out Butler's words as the world around him was systematically drained of color.

That's when he saw it—a long, slender shape standing almost as tall as the ceiling. It had long, white limbs, and in the gray haze he could see the indentations of a face. Whatever it was, it had eyes, a nose, and a mouth. The lanky, wretched thing lingered in the gray gloom, watching the four of them from its corner.

He realized he could no longer see Butler's features, nor could he understand anything the man said. His voice came through as a garbled mess, and Donovan could only make out the man's dark gray outline. The same was true of the two Tammys, who made various quips and asides throughout Butler's conversation, but Donovan could not understand a damn word of it.

The scrawny, albino *thing* swayed lazily in the corner, shifting its weight from one foot to the other. Its knuckles brushed the slate floor with long, slow strokes. Donovan watched, his face locked into an expression of confusion, fear.

I'm insane. He admitted it to himself. His heart beat a heavy tattoo in his chest, and sweat ran from his pores. *I've lost my mind.*

In that moment he realized just how limitless the depths of his insanity truly were. The thing *noticed* him. Its swaying ceased as it planted its full weight on both feet. It cocked its head in his direction, raised one, spindly arm, and beckoned to him with a loud, forlorn moan.

-3-
GRAY SIGHT

A RIPPLE RAN through the thing's pale flesh. It squinted its empty, black eyes and kept pointing at him with one spindly finger.

Donovan's heart raced. Was this real? How could it possibly be? It defied his grasp of logic, tickling a place down in his brain, a place he used to call his imagination. This was a figment of his own creation, a repressed idea manifesting in the form of a waking nightmare. He *had* lost his mind—and this was his body's way of telling him.

He blinked. The room went back to normal. Butler and the Tammys were still in their seats, each one sounding off a number which, at first, did not make any sense to him. He was still distracted by what had just happened. It was a hallucination. Had to be. It was a chemical imbalance in his brain, maybe, or perhaps a side effect of a head trauma he could not remember. These possibilities plagued him so much that when Butler called his name, he jumped from his seat.

"Whoa, easy there. Are you okay, Candle?"

Donovan stared at his superiors, then back to the corner of the room. He expected the lanky creature to be there, but it wasn't. He went back to his chair, and the tension slowly leaked from the room, replaced by dread.

"I'm sorry," he said, clearing his throat. He felt as if he'd swallowed sandpaper. "What were you saying?"

Timothy Butler chuckled and said, "Overall we gave you a 3.8."

Donovan's eye twitched. He forgot about his bizarre hallucinations. A 3.8? What kind of number was 3.8? Never in his nine years had they given him anything but a whole number, which was usually a four. But 3.8? He repeated it to himself. Three. Point. Eight. It implied he'd done worse this year than the last, which made no sense to him—after all, he'd worked harder this year than any other. He could understand receiving a 4.8, but this? No, this would not stand.

"A three-point-eight?"

"Yeah," Butler said, gathering his files together. He stood and finished off a cup of coffee. "New ranking system. Nifty, huh?"

"But a 3.8?"

"Is there a problem, Mr. Candle?" Tammy Q. frowned.

He cleared his throat, stared at his blinking hands, and said, "Problem? N-No, no problem. I was just . . ."

Tammy P. strained to look at him. She forced a smile. "Yes?"

"The score seems a little low, is all. I thought I worked very hard this year."

"And you have, Candle!" Butler chuckled. "We just see it as a means of incentive. Right, ladies?"

The Tammys nodded.

"Incentive?"

"That's right. For you to work harder and strive for even more excellence." Butler stood and opened the door. He wore that same, conniving grin from the day before. Seeing it made Donovan's blood pressure rise.

"Besides, there's always room for improvement!"

With that, Timothy Butler left the room. The Tammys whispered among themselves. Tammy P. giggled at something Tammy Q. said, but Donovan could not hear what passed between them. After a moment, he cleared his throat and spoke.

"Was there something else?" Donovan asked. They looked

up at him, startled by the sound of his voice, and looked in his direction. Tammy Q. chewed her bottom lip as she strained to look at him.

The room shifted back to gray for an instant. Donovan saw a second, lanky figure standing behind the two women. Then things returned to normal. Tammy P. spoke.

"Just a teensy-tiny thing," she said.

"Your salary increase," Tammy Q. added.

Donovan nodded. "Which is?"

"Since your performance score falls into the median bracket, you're eligible for the standard quarter-per-hour increase."

His stomach lurched once again. He tried to ignore it as he rolled their words in his head. A quarter. Twenty-five cents. A year of kissing ass and working self-imposed double-time was worth a quarter? Donovan opened his mouth to speak, but his vision went gray once more. The sensation in his stomach grew to a sharp jolt. The room flashed, and that prickly feeling crawled across his skin. One of the Tammys spoke, but her voice was slow and garbled.

Donovan forgot about the measly raise. His attention turned to the pair of long, tall albino figures standing in the room with them. They stood in place, swaying in tandem, their elongated arms touching the ground. Their black, empty eyes looked upon him with unflinching apathy. He was but an insect to them, a passing curiosity.

The second figure stepped toward the gray table. Donovan's heart beat furiously in his chest. What were these things? And why did he see them? His imagination filled in the gaps. *Ghosts*, he thought, *or demons—*

"—any questions, Mr. Candle?"

Color flooded back into the room, and he found himself staring at Tammy Perpa. He couldn't bring himself to speak—how could he? His mind raced with impossibilities, all of which seemed alien. Spirits? Invisibility? These things weren't possible. This was reality, and—

"Mr. Candle?"

"Y-Yes?" he asked at once, eyes darting between the two women.

"Do you have any questions?

He shook his head without thinking. The Tammys stood and collected their things.

"Good!" they said together, then giggled at their sickening uniformity. Donovan watched them leave the room. When they were gone, he closed his eyes and buried his face in his hands.

My God, what next? he wondered. *What next?*

•

Donovan spent the next few days wandering in a stupor. The befuddlement of Tuesday morning continued throughout the week, and all the while he tried to rationalize the strange, transparent disease afflicting his body. Tuesday night, when he went to urinate, he caught sight of his own manhood blinking out of existence. For that brief instance he saw only an arc of urine flow into the toilet. He screamed and succeeded in soiling himself.

Donna ignored his distress. He made great effort to communicate with his wife, only to be met with silence. The few times she did acknowledge his presence was to reciprocate the staples "I love you" and "Good night." Even then, he saw the confusion on her face, as though she hadn't noticed his presence until those precise moments.

He wanted to believe it was a dream, that he would wake up Wednesday morning and discover it was still Tuesday. He imagined waking to find his life the same as before, full of hope and color. Maybe Donna wouldn't give him the cold shoulder, would make him a nice breakfast, would kiss him on the cheek again when he came home.

But when he woke the next morning, all was not well with his world. He rose at the same time and found himself in the midst of grayness. It shifted back to normal as he rubbed the sleep from his eyes. He got up, frowned at himself in the mirror, and went about his morning ritual.

Downstairs, he watched in silence as Donna made herself some toast and took a seat at the table. He sat across from her, watching her mannerisms, waiting for her to acknowledge his presence. She did not look up from her breakfast.

Frustrated, Donovan opened the morning newspaper and

flipped through its pages. A photograph caught his eye. It was of a young woman with an intense stare. HAVE YOU SEEN ME? it asked. Her name was Alice Walenta, and he recognized it from a radio ad the day before. How quickly he'd dismissed it, caught up in the rush of the morning traffic and hopes of impressing his superiors. He considered how easy it was for someone to vanish without a trace. *Maybe I'm going to disappear*, he thought. The possibility was frightening.

The photograph, with Ms. Walenta's dark eyes rendered grainy and pale by the newsprint, made him anxious. A deep hum rose up from within his head, causing a slow throb at his temples. He looked away from the photograph. The hum stopped, and the room around him shifted, losing its color. The kitchen's gray tones deepened, its cabinetry and appliances losing their texture, becoming nothing more than blank slates of empty geometry. Donna's figure became a shadow, and that's when he saw it.

A tiny, white figure emerged from behind Donna's head. It was small, no taller than a few inches, its flesh seemingly rubbery, glistening in the dim un-light of the room. It was bipedal, standing on two stubby legs, hands settled on what might have been its hips. He stared at it, unblinking, unable to move—not out of fear, but out of shock. Just when Donovan thought he'd reached the bottom of his sanity, the floor dropped out from underneath, spilling him further into its depths.

The white thing bent at the knees and sat next to Donna's ear. It leaned over, put its head against her earlobe, and spoke in a droning language he could not understand. To Donovan's ears, it sounded like a record played in reverse, tinged with the electronic interference of a bad phone connection.

The kitchen flickered and slowly lost its gray hue. Donna's features regained their definition. For a few seconds both realities overlapped, and Donovan could see the white thing sitting beside her head. She chewed on her toast, unaware of its presence.

Words found their way up the back of Donovan's throat. They came forth from his lips in a single, incredulous spate.

"What the hell is this?"

The white thing took notice of him. It looked at him with two black, beady eyes, and said something else into Donna's ear. She kept staring at the table.

"Get off her," Donovan said, reaching forward to knock the pale thing from her shoulder. His fingers passed through it. Donna did not move. The white thing grinned at him, extended its thin, white hand, and gave him the finger.

He scoffed. *Fuck you, too.*

The overlap of color and gray subsided with another flash. Donovan ignored the prickling of his skin as his kitchen returned to normal. He watched the creature fade from view. Even when it was gone, he could still feel it leering at him.

For the first time since the affliction began, Donovan wondered if what he saw was not a figment of his imagination, but a reality. *No*, he thought, *things like this don't happen.* Even if they did, the odds of it happening to him were astronomical. Things like this did not happen to Donovan Candle. He'd written about things like this, sure, but for the precise reason that they *couldn't* happen, least of all to him.

Donovan got up from the table. He looked at Donna, unsure of himself and his sanity. He reached out and put his hand on her shoulder, expecting to feel the form of that creature, rendered invisible by the kitchen's lively color. His hand landed upon her shoulder. She was warm.

Donna looked up at him, smiled and said, "I love you, too. Have a nice day at work, dear."

"I didn't—" he began, then remembered the thing on her shoulder. He remembered the way it whispered its backward language into her ear. Was it filling in the blanks? Was it the reason she couldn't understand him?

He glanced at the clock, saw he was running late, and made his way to the door. He stopped short, looked back at Donna. She flipped through the newspaper.

"Love you," he said, and closed the door behind him. He didn't see her recoil at the sound of his voice.

•

He agonized over the morning's incident for the rest of the day. At work, even as he read the sales prompt to a stranger on the line, his mind wandered back to Donna. He could see the white thing on her shoulder every time he closed his eyes. When a potential customer hung up on him, he removed his headset and retreated to the men's room. He had no urge to go, but this was his most private place to sit and think.

Donovan closed the door, locked it, and sat on the toilet.

You can figure this out, he told himself. *There's a logical, reasonable explanation. There has to be.* To this argument, Joe Hopper replied, *Only logic I see in this is that you're crazy, hoss. How's that sound?*

He didn't like it one bit. The alternative prospect was also one that filled him with dread. What if he truly were disappearing? What if these things he saw were real? The little thing on Donna's shoulder was bad enough, but the big ones that lurked in the corners of the office conference room terrified him. A chill slowly worked its way down his back.

When he returned to his cubicle, he saw he'd been gone for almost a full hour. There were no messages waiting for him in his inbox or on his phone. Given all that had happened—and all that *was* happening—he was not surprised. First his wife ignored him, and now his coworkers. With enough time, everyone just might forget he existed.

That thought left a sour taste in his mouth. He looked around the sales floor. His stomach twisted into itself as the room was overlapped by its gray counterpart. Other salespeople became dark shades, and he saw more of the little white things sitting on their shoulders. They turned their bulbous, white heads in a single, uniform motion. Their beady eyes looked at him, into him. *Through* him.

Donovan flickered back into reality. The office returned to its normal, colorful state. He sat and put on his headset, determined to ignore the impossible things he'd witnessed. Unlike those in his immediate presence, the strangers to whom he spoke over the phone lines always seemed to hear him just fine.

"Seriously, man, don't you ever get bored?"

"Sometimes."

"I'd say all the time, from the sound of it. Do you always call customers sounding like this?"

"Like what?"

"Like you've had the shit kicked out of you six ways to Sunday. Seriously, you sound like you're completely drained. How long have you been doing this?"

"Nine years."

"Wow. I dunno, dude. That's a long time to be making calls to strangers. Did you go to college?"

"I did. Haven't thought about that in a long time, though."

"Didn't you have any goals? Any dreams?"

"Yeah. I wanted to be a writer."

"I can dig that, man. Well hey, I gotta go, but look, dude, don't waste your life there, okay? Go write something. Realize your dream."

"Yeah," Donovan sighed, "I'll get right on that."

"Cool, cool. Oh, and thanks for the introductory offer, but I don't think I need to protect my identity right now. Peace."

Click. Beep.

The script for saving a sale lingered on his tongue. *No one ever wants to protect their identity until it's taken from them.* Donovan cancelled the automated dialer before it could place another call. He ran his hands through his hair. Dozens of calls, and not a single sale. At this point he did not care.

What could he do about the gray visions and his own untimely disappearance? To whom could he turn?

Michael crossed his mind. He imagined working with his brother to track down the cause of the phenomenon. Twin detectives. The notion stirred a dying ember of creativity in his mind.

Yeah, right. Michael may have been his inspiration for Joe Hopper, but he was hardly empathetic. Michael Candle was more likely to laugh at his plight than help him. That was, of course, presuming his brother could even see or hear him.

Donovan put away the thought of calling Michael. He was desperate, but not *that* desperate. This was something he had to figure out on his own.

His body shimmered. The color drained from his vision. He caught a glimpse of the lanky, white figure standing between two cubicles along the far wall. It saw him, took a series of steps down the aisle, and was gone in a blink. The office bustled around him with full, vibrant life. He checked his watch, gathered his things, and made his way out of the building.

By the time he got to his car he'd forgotten all about his brother. Whatever was happening to him, he understood he would have to handle it on his own—and that, above everything else, frightened him most.

-4-
THE OMITTED

THE DAYS GREW worse. He saw more of the tall, white things and their Lilliputian counterparts. On Wednesday night he happened to look outside and spot a lanky one on the sidewalk. He turned away from the bedroom window and looked at Donna, but in the midst of the gray sight she was nothing more than a dark specter shrouded in the blankets.

When he turned back he saw the creature beckon to him with a long, scrawny finger. Its mouth shivered open as it uttered a low moan.

It vanished as color returned. Donna was already fast asleep. He tried to snuggle next to her—after all, it was their night to make love and attempt to conceive a child. She rolled away from him. Defeated, Donovan turned on his side and fell into a troubling sleep in which he was haunted by nightmares of the white creatures. In his dream, they chased him down a long, gray staircase. It wasn't until the albino things were upon him that he realized his efforts were futile. The staircase was really an escalator, delivering him straight into their pale, skinny hands.

Donovan woke Thursday morning drenched in sweat and

twenty minutes late. Donna was already downstairs, and like the day before, she did not acknowledge his presence. When the gray sight overcame his vision, he saw the little white bastard sitting atop Donna's shoulder. Its head was pressed against her ear, and he could hear its backward chatter.

"Stop it." He wished his voice didn't sound so weak. The creature's head twisted around. It grinned, revealing a set of prickly teeth, and *winked* at him.

The kitchen returned to normal. Donna did not look up at him. She ate her breakfast and read the newspaper in silence. He left that morning without saying goodbye, and found that things at work hadn't changed, either.

At lunch time, rather than sit in the lounge, he spent an hour in the men's room trying to sort out his troubled life. *What if this is permanent?* he wondered, to which Joe Hopper responded, *What makes you think it ain't, boss?*

Donovan considered it a fair point. The symptoms of whatever was happening were getting worse. He was isolated now, living among the rest of the world while being omitted from it. The visions, and the question of whether or not they were real, were growing more and more prevalent as well. His "gray sight" revealed monstrosities the likes of which he could never fathom on his own. They were creatures suited for more fortified minds, fictional beings culled from a mind far more creative than his own.

Logic and reason had failed him, left in the past with Monday and some semblance of reality. He wondered if his soul would fade away with the rest of him. He wondered if Donna would remember him once he was gone.

That's enough. I'll find a way through this.

He left the restroom strengthened by his determination, but as the day wore on, he wasn't entirely sure he believed it.

•

A five-car pileup on the highway made him almost an hour late for dinner. Donna was finished with her meal by the time he arrived home. He tried to apologize and explain himself, but it was in vain. She could neither hear him or see him. What troubled him most about it was that she didn't seem to miss him, and it was then he remembered the crude thing on her shoulder for the last two mornings. He remembered the way it whispered it in her ear, the way it mocked him.

Were the white things at the root of all this? If they were, then all of this—the flickering, the gray visions, the tall creatures—were very much a part of reality. It meant there was something far more sinister at work than just the gradual breakdown of his sanity.

Donovan chose not to dwell on it, locking himself away in his office to work on his novel. He struggled for half an hour as he tried to begin again, but his mind kept wandering back to the matters at hand. *How would Joe Hopper solve this?* he wondered. *Or Michael Candle, for that matter?* He looked at the phone, contemplated picking it up and calling his brother, but feared he would be met with more silence. Just because the unwitting customers at work could hear him did not mean anyone else could.

He went to bed early and tried to sleep away his trouble. His thoughts kept him awake, and he laid there for an hour before Donna crawled into bed beside him. She usually kissed him goodnight, but for the last two nights she had not, and tonight was no different. If his suspicions were correct, he could not blame her for this, but it still stung him.

Donovan needed his wife now more than ever. Throughout their years of marriage she'd always been his right hand, his navigator, and closest friend. Even though her sudden inability to acknowledge his existence gave credence to his earlier fears that he was slowly being omitted from the world, it did not make the rejection any easier.

He spent the next hour crying into his pillow.

•

Friday morning was much like the three mornings before it. He woke, experienced the gut-pulling transition between color and gray realities, and saw creatures that should not exist outside the realm of fiction. Donna ignored him, as did his co-workers. By eleven o'clock he'd made it through a block of calls, and so far it seemed those total strangers were the only ones who paid him any attention.

It made little sense to him that they could hear him when those around him could not, but by this point Donovan didn't care. He was happy to have some form of interaction, whether they were shouting, screaming, crying, or simply talking to him. Even in their hatred for an annoying sales rep, Donovan found some kind of hope in their frustrations. He welcomed them.

In an effort to connect with his audience, if only for a few moments, Donovan abandoned the standard Identinel sales script. Instead he interacted with his potential customers, engaging them in all manner of conversation. What else did he have to lose?

All topics were fair game. If he connected with the right person, the conversation could last for up to an hour. One call went to a woman in Iowa named Eileen Carmike. For forty-seven minutes and fifty-three seconds, she and Donovan held a conversation about philosophy and the proper way to bake a turkey. Another call went to an elderly gentleman in Oregon named Zachary Rosen who had a passion for old cars and The Grateful Dead.

Though he enjoyed these conversations, Donovan grew increasingly depressed as he realized what he was missing from life. Here were people living their lives, with their own quirks and faults, and yet they were still somehow perfectly content. After a call with young Jimmy Frank, and their strange conversation about the nature of first and last names, Donovan removed the headset and checked his watch.

It was 4:30. He had time for one more call before braving traffic for another silent night at home. He rubbed his eyes, yawned, and put on the headset. The automated dialer generated a new phone number with a single keystroke.

Click. Beep.

A sharp hiss of static surged through the earphone. He cringed. It reminded him of an old dial-up modem. The surge devolved into the normal series of rings, followed by an abrupt connection. No one spoke on the other end.

Donovan paused. The monitor revealed no name or address. All information fields were blank.

"Hello? Anyone there?"

More electronic interference shot through the line and took

shape as a man's voice. It was a steady voice, confident but soft-spoken. A whine of digital noise hung in the background.

"Hello. Who is this?"

Donovan cleared his throat. "My name is Donovan Candle, and I'm a sales rep for Identinel Security Services. You may have seen our commercials—"

"I have not. What is the nature of your business?"

"We offer identity theft protection. Do you mind if I give you a sales pitch?"

"I find it ironic that a man of little identity is offering to protect the identity of others. How . . . *noble.*"

Donovan said nothing. He wasn't sure how to respond to that.

"In lieu of a sales pitch," said the nameless man, "I would not mind hearing a life pitch from you."

A life pitch?

"I'm sorry," Donovan said, "but I'm not sure I understand what you mean."

"Please forgive my poor manners. You just sound like a man who is not getting all he wants out of life. Tell me, Mr. Candle, what do you want out of your life?"

His mouth was parched. It was rare a customer turned the tables on him so effectively. He had years of experience in dealing with this sort of thing. There were ways to direct a conversation back on track, but Donovan suddenly found he lacked the desire. Something about the man unnerved him, but his curiosity pushed him to answer.

"It's not every day I'm asked that question. Let's see . . ."

"You do not have to answer that now, Mr. Candle. It was rhetorical."

"No, sir, it's perfectly fine. My life has taken a strange turn these last few days. To be honest, I'm not really sure what I want out of life anymore. Today, after talking to other folks like yourself, I've realized just how much I'm missing."

"Missing?"

"In life. There's not much that defines me anymore. I guess if something interesting doesn't happen to me soon, I may disappear for good." An uncomfortable silence followed his words. The static on the line rose and fell, accenting a low chuckle from the strange man beyond it.

"Do you really think so?"

"Yeah," Donovan said. "I do. Just a feeling, really."

"Actions birth definition, Mr. Candle. Good luck finding your way."

Click.

•

"So how are things?"

Donna Candle juggled the phone and a mixing bowl. She set the bowl on the counter. Her sister, Amanda, waited on the other end of the line for a response.

"That's a loaded question and you know it."

"Oh, please. It is *not*. You've bitched about Don all week."

She reached into the cupboard and retrieved a bag of flour. "I haven't *bitched*. I'm just concerned, is all. He's never behaved like this."

"I don't know, Donna. From what you've told me, it seems pretty damn suspicious."

Donna sighed. She regretted ever saying anything to her sister about Donovan's odd behavior.

"I trust my husband, Amanda, so don't go putting any ideas in my head. There's something going on, but I doubt it's what you think it is."

"If you say so. You know the man better than anyone."

"I do," Donna said, and trailed off. *I thought I did.* She'd run the gamut of emotion and suspicion in response to Donovan's silence. At first she wondered if there was someone else, but he wouldn't do something like that. Not the man she knew, anyway. In recent days, however, it was difficult for her to keep those agonizing doubts at bay.

"Donnie's no cheat," Donna said. She smiled. "He knows what I'd do to him if he ever did."

Amanda laughed. "Out come the scissors. Oh, hey—I should get going. Quinn just got home."

"Give my love to my favorite nephew," Donna said.

"I will. And hang in there, okay? Call if you need me."

They said their goodbyes. Donna hung up the phone and looked at the mixing bowl. After spending most of the day in a restless fervor, she decided she would bake a chocolate cake—from scratch, with peanut butter icing. It was Donovan's favorite, and would serve as her olive branch. She couldn't stand for him to be mad at her. She'd gone over every possible reason as to why he would act in such a manner toward her, and their argument was the only logical solution.

It didn't help that she had been plagued by sporadic migraines all week. That was another odd thing. The headaches came out of nowhere, in strange, buzzing surges that filled her head with a dull, blinding pain. They made it hard to concentrate on anything, and always erupted at the most inopportune moments.

She'd tried explaining it to Donovan, but he was distant and quiet. Some nights she thought he was with her in the living room, but when she would look over, his chair would be empty. Sometimes, when he was there, he said strange things that didn't make sense, but she couldn't remember what they were. She went to bed alone, and her concerns grew as the days went by.

Had she gone too far? The more she strained to remember the details of their argument, the more they seemed to slip away. She remembered her tone, and regretted it. She remembered the gist of what she'd said, and that it was honest. She was tired of always saving, always scrimping for a goal that he kept pushing farther back. It disappointed her, seeing her husband slowly transform into the man he was, when she remembered how vibrant and lively he was in college.

Donna smiled. Those were better days. She loved Donovan with all her heart—always would—but she admitted to herself that this week tested her resolve. It simply wasn't like him to ignore her. That morning he hadn't even said goodbye. She'd called her sister to vent, and now suspected Amanda was already on the phone with their mother, spilling the latest gossip.

One of the headaches crept into her forehead. She winced, steadied herself against the kitchen counter, and waited for it to subside.

When the migraine passed, she looked at the clock. Donovan would be home in an hour. She turned on the radio and went about preparing his cake.

There came a knock at the door. Donna turned down the radio, listening. They were quick knocks, paced evenly in threes.

Knock-knock-knock.

She wiped flour from her hands and left the kitchen. There was a man at the door, his features distorted by its segmented windows. He wore a suit. *Great*, she thought, *a salesman.*

Donna unlocked the door, and pulled it open. When she saw the look in his eye, she caught the door with her foot, wishing she'd not opened it. There was something wrong about him, the way he looked at her, and it was even more apparent when she saw his clothes. He wore a large, green coat over a tattered suit. His tie was torn in half and hung limp, its threaded entrails stretching the length of his stained, white shirt. His hair was long and matted, peppered with slick, silver strands. The thick lenses of his glasses were smudged, giving his large eyes a cloudy appearance. He could've been a salesman, if he wasn't so dirty.

Her breath caught in her throat. The smell was terrible. The man looked beyond her, into the kitchen. Donna tightened her grip on the doorknob.

"Afternoon, ma'am."

"Can I help you?" She forced a smile. The stench made her eyes water.

"Are you Donna Candle?"

"Yes," she said. His eyes darted back and forth, focusing on her and something behind her. She cleared her throat. "Can I help you, mister?"

His lips curved into a nervous smile, and before she could react, his hand was on the door. He shoved his weight against it with such force that it sent her sprawling. The room danced for a moment as she fell, and when she collapsed, the world went dark.

•

Donovan caught the middle of another interview with Dr. Albert Sparrow while inching along the highway. As traffic ground to another stand-still, Donovan turned up the volume to drown out the surrounding noise of idling engines and horn blasts.

"—sometimes, when we're at our very limit, we may find ourselves in what I have labeled a *state of liminality*."

"Liminality?" asked the host.

The line of cars in front lurched forward a few more inches. Donovan flickered, and for a span of seconds he saw the white figures wandering between the rows of traffic.

"Yes, liminality. A state of transition. Think of it as if you were standing in a doorway, with one foot inside and one foot out."

"So you're saying mediocrity places us 'in the doorway,' so to speak?"

"Something like that, yes. In this so-called doorway, a person stands on the threshold of two states—one of complete, dissolute anonymity, and one of profound activity. In my book, I—"

Here comes the sales pitch, Donovan mused. He switched off the radio. Traffic eased up, and ten minutes later he pulled into his driveway. He parked the car, took a breath, and approached the door. On a whim, he called out to Donna as he turned the knob and stepped inside.

"Honey, I'm—"

His voice failed him, his brain refusing to accept the message relayed by his eyes. For a moment, every mental function shut down, and he forgot to breathe. His aborted greeting echoed across the entrance and into the kitchen. He had an unobstructed view of the disarray. Once his mind thawed enough to allow simple thought processes, he began to absorb all that he saw.

The garbage can was on its side, leaving trash strewn across the tile floor. Package wrappers, soda cans, and potato peels mingled with an overturned canister of flour and a puddle of milk. Some eggs remained on the counter, while others were crushed into a runny, yellow amalgam on the floor. Donna's mixing bowl sat on the counter next to a jar of peanut butter.

What the hell happened?

He imagined Donna in the process of baking something when

all this happened. He took a step forward and saw the scattered pattern of footprints in the dusting of flour. A cold shard of ice shot down the length of his spine.

It was the ensemble of cutlery scattered across the floor at the end of the room that finally jarred him from his panic. The wooden block, home to all of Donna's sharp knives, was overturned in front of the refrigerator door. His blood pressure rose as he looked at their chaotic placement across the tile. His heart beat a tribal call in his chest. He knew from the assortment that there weren't enough knives. Some of them were missing.

In his panic, Donna's name became a constant thrum, creating an inner vibration that urged him to move.

"Donna?" he called out. He didn't like the sound of his voice. It sounded too small, too weak, and he realized it didn't matter because she probably couldn't hear him, anyway.

Might be best shut your mouth, boss. S'pose you ain't alone?

If he wasn't alone, then who might still be in the house with him? His imagination built the scenario. Donna was preparing to bake a cake when someone—man or woman, it didn't matter—burst into the room, catching her off guard, and—

He looked at the knives again. The mental scenario played on in the back of his head. He pictured a person in a black ski mask lurking in their bedroom closet. Donna was on the bed, bound, and gagged. Seeing her there in such a state, he would rush in with his guard down, and then—

He swallowed, and his throat clicked. His heart beat with such force that his whole body shook. Donovan blinked. He knelt, plucking a steak knife from the floor, and followed signs of the struggle into the dining room.

Donovan froze. Blood dotted the table cloth. He moved along the edge of the table, whispering a silent prayer that it didn't belong to his wife. A lump rose in his throat, making breathing difficult.

He saw Mr. Precious Paws on the other side of the table, and his legs gave out. He fell to his knees and found that he could not blink. The first thing that came to mind was a simple, absurd thought: *So that's what happened to the knives.*

Mr. Precious Paws lay sprawled on the floor, the largest of

Donna's butcher knives buried in his back. Another jutted out the back of the cat's neck, indicated by a stream of arterial spray that hit the opposing wall and formed a dark trail leading back to the dead animal. Mr. Precious Paws' eyes were dilated, affixed on a point in space beyond the room. He looked terrified.

Donovan bit his lower lip and grimaced at the taste of bile at the back of his throat. His efforts couldn't last, and he retched.

"Mr. Precious Paws," he whimpered. The reality of the situation struck him. "Oh God, Donna!"

Blinded by panic, Donovan dropped the knife as he scrambled out of the room and up the stairs. He called out to his wife as he ran, his heart exploding in his chest. He threw open the bedroom door, ignorant of the scenario concocted by his imagination. She wasn't on the bed, nor was there a masked man waiting to ambush him.

"*Donna!*" He screamed until his throat burned, the words scratching their way out of him like a frightened animal. The bathroom was empty, as were the office and spare bedroom at the end of the hall. *Donna*, his mind raced. *Donna, Donna, Donna.* Spots of black and purple blossomed across his field of vision, and he teetered on his feet.

When the splotches of color dimmed, Donovan found himself filled with a new urgency. The cops. He had to call the cops. On his way into the office, he realized he'd trampled right through the crime scene. *They'll get over it, boss.* Hopper's words cooled him. He sucked in his breath and reached for the phone—when it rang.

It startled him. He looked at the black cordless as though he'd never seen it before, its screen lighting up to say UNKNOWN CALLER. Donovan pressed TALK. He lifted it to his ear and tried to speak, but his quivering jaw did not make it easy. The tears were already streaming down his face.

"H-Hello?"

A hiss of electronic noise filled his ears, and the drone took shape as a man's voice.

"Hello, Mr. Candle."

He recognized the soft-spoken voice. Realization spread through him in the form of a chill. The hairs on his arms and neck stood at attention. He shook so badly that he almost dropped the phone. *How?* he wondered. *How could that man get my number?* He had to hang up and call the police. He didn't have time for this, he had to—

"Are you with me, Mr. Candle?"

Donovan dry-swallowed. "I'm here."

"Good." The nameless man chuckled. "How is *this* for interesting, Mr. Candle?"

For an instant, the man's reference was lost on him, but it all came racing back to Donovan in a heated reverie: *I guess if something interesting doesn't happen to me soon, I may disappear for good.*

Everything clicked. An icy feeling settled in the bottom of his gut.

More electronic noise filled the line. When it subsided, the man was chuckling again. It made Donovan's heart stop.

The unknown caller's voice changed, imbued with the white noise of the line.

"Is this interesting enough for you?"

-5-
PUPPETS

Donovan gaped into the phone. Words failed him.

"Well, Mr. Candle?"

The stark, electronic buzz rose up again, accenting the man's words. Donovan gripped the phone while thoughts raced laps around his head.

"Who the hell are you?" he rasped.

"There will be time for introductions later, Mr. Candle. Please answer my question."

Donna, he thought. *Oh God, Donna, what has he done to you?* A thick cloud of heat surrounded his face. Donovan's knees buckled, and he sank into his office chair.

"Mr. Candle."

"What question? Look, I—"

"Is this interesting enough for you?"

He swallowed air. The lump tightened in his throat. "Yes."

"Good." The soft-spoken man seemed pleased. His tone lightened, now almost jovial. "Allow me to introduce myself. My name is Aleister Dullington."

Donovan closed his eyes. "Mr. Dullington, did you take my

wife? Did you hurt her?"

"Do not despair, Mr. Candle. I assure you that your wife is quite safe—for now."

For now. The bottom dropped out of Donovan's gut. *Keep it together, hoss.*

"Where is she?"

"In due time."

Donovan shot out of his seat. The words were out of his mouth before he could stop them.

"You tell me where she is, you son of a bitch. You tell me *now*."

"Now, now, Mr. Candle. It is not wise to curse the one who determines whether your precious Donna lives or dies."

The sudden rush of adrenaline left him. He felt weak, feeble. He sank back into his chair and closed his eyes. *Whether your precious Donna lives or dies.* The words tumbled and spun in his head, bouncing off images of the kitchen and dead cat. *He's hurt her, oh God, he's hurt her or he's going to hurt her, or—*

"Calm yourself, Mr. Candle. What I have to tell you will be most displeasing."

Sweat dotted his forehead. The air in the room was suddenly very suffocating. Donovan took it all in with one prolonged breath. He held it in his chest, letting it burn through his lungs, before slowly exhaling. His heart calmed.

"I'm listening."

"You are a boring man, Mr. Candle."

"Boring?" he snorted. His wife was missing, and this guy on the line had the gall to *criticize* him? "Where is Donna? I want to talk to her right *now*—"

"I ask for your patience, Mr. Candle." Aleister Dullington remained calm, his voice reflecting no emotion. He spoke in measured syllables, with a flat intensity which ran beneath every vowel and consonant. "Do not push me. *Or else.*"

Donovan shut his mouth. He tried to ignore the thoughts racing through his head, and took another deep breath. He held it inside longer than the last one.

"You are boring. You have spent the last nine years of your life in a job that stifles you. You slave toward empty goals making empty promises to yourself and your wife."

"Mister, I don't need your insults."

"These are not insults, Mr. Candle, these are truths. If you find them insulting, I implore you to consider why that might be."

Donovan choked back a bitter reply.

"The transparency afflicting you is what I refer to as the 'flickering.' It is the result of your supersaturation with mediocrity."

"What?" The exasperation in his own voice startled him. "Listen, asshole, I don't know about you, but I've had enough of this bullsh—"

"Mr. Candle, if you interrupt me again, I will see to it that your wife's non-vital organs are separated from her body." His voice darkened, tinged with electronic resonance that made the phone hiss. "We will start with her ovaries."

Donovan fought back tears. His mounting frustration broke and withered under the man's threat.

"Do I have your undivided attention now, Mr. Candle?"

"Yes."

"Good. Your life is saturated with mediocrity. As a result, you are flickering out. You are experiencing odd things, seeing things that should not be, your vision reduced to shades of gray."

"Yeah."

"Indeed. You are seeing the world behind the world, a place I call the Monochrome. This is where you will end up, should you fail to cure your banality."

His head spun. The strange man's words tumbled through his mind as he tried to process everything. Monochrome? A world behind the world? The words sounded ridiculous when spoken aloud, and Donovan would have discounted them as the ramblings of a mad man had he not experienced things exactly as Dullington described them.

But there was something else, something far worse than his own absurd affliction. Donna was gone, and Dullington was behind it. That was all Donovan needed to make him forget himself. It was all about Donna now, flickering be damned.

"Are you still with me, Mr. Candle?"

"I am."

"You may speak. I am eager to hear your response." Aleister Dullington's voice was cold, proper. Professional.

"What have you done with my wife?" The words numbed his lips.

"Mrs. Candle is well."

"Answer my question." His temper rose, but he tried his best to keep it under control. To ignite Dullington's own fuse, which he suspected was quite short, would be a grave error—not just for Donna, but for himself.

"Your ire is encouraging." The upward pitch in Dullington's voice gave Donovan the image of a smile on an otherwise expressionless face. He couldn't fathom how someone could smile in such a situation, but then again, this man hardly seemed normal.

"I like a good show, Mr. Candle, and you seem like a man with the potential to deliver. For this reason alone, I offer you an opportunity to redeem yourself." He paused. Static filled the line for a moment, then subsided. "Forgive me. You asked a question, and I will answer. Your wife is bound ankle and wrist. A bag covers her head. Before you ask, Mr. Candle, no. No one has had their way with her—yet."

Donovan clenched his teeth at that last detail. Thinking of Donna in such a predicament made his helplessness in the matter even more unbearable. He pictured her smiling face instead.

"Go on," he said.

"As to where she is, I am afraid I cannot tell you right now. All you need to know is that she is safe, and as comfortable as her situation allows."

"Why are you doing this to her?" His throat clicked when he swallowed, and he fought against the nausea stirring in his stomach.

Dullington went on, ignoring Donovan's question. "I am a reaper of boredom, Mr. Candle, I feed on it. It is my sustenance, and the Monochrome—the world behind your world—is *my* realm. The flickering brings you here."

Donovan thought of the visions, the white creatures lurking in the gray haze. Was this what he had to look forward to? Was this "Monochrome" his final destination? *This is crazy*, he thought. *Absolute lunacy.*

"The irony," Dullington said, "is that this diet of boredom grows tedious." The connection swelled with wheezing, digitized static. "I yearn for the entertainment you take for granted."

Donovan hesitated, "You're . . . bored with boredom?"

"Precisely. I knew you were bright, which is why I offer you a second chance. If you do not change your predicament, Mr. Candle, you will flicker out. Most people will not miss you. Some will, but only after it is too late. However, I am willing to offer you a task. Complete it, and earn yourself a second chance."

"What task?" Donovan swallowed. His throat was suddenly very dry, scratchy.

"I have lost someone very important to me. Find him, return him, and I will return Mrs. Candle to you. In the process, your exploits entertain me. It is a win-win situation, so to speak. Agreed?"

"But—" he began, then paused. He considered hanging up the phone and dialing 911, but what would he say? And what could the police do? He feared that doing so would result in repercussions for Donna. He felt trapped. This stranger had complete authority over the situation, over his life, and over Donna's. The ball was in Dullington's court, and Donovan would have to play by his rules—however preposterous—or forfeit.

"Time is running out, Mr. Candle, I must be going. But I will tell you one thing: the man who kidnapped your wife is at a diner called Rossetti's."

Donovan's heart sank, and he once again fought the urge to vomit. The taste of bile filled his mouth, and his stomach burned. Rossetti's, where he and Donna had their first date. He felt a deep hatred for the man on the phone. Though he'd never considered himself a violent person, he wanted nothing more than to wrap his fingers around Dullington's throat and squeeze.

"His name is George Guffin, and he is waiting for you there. I have instructed him to guide you onward. Do you understand?"

"Yes, but—" Donovan began, cut off by a low, pulsing drone of noise that surged through the line. It sounded like heavy, digital breathing. "—but who *are* you?"

The drone went on. Through it, Dullington spoke. "Who are *you*, Mr. Candle?"

He wasn't sure how to respond. The question probed far deeper than he cared to explore at the moment. There were more pressing matters at hand.

"You do not have to answer now, Mr. Candle, but you will before this is over."

There was a crush of static, then the deafening silence of a disconnect. In the solitude of his office, Donovan Candle hung up the phone, buried his face in his hands, and cried.

•

His mind shut down, and for an indeterminable span of time Donovan sat and stared off into space. *Think*, he ordered himself. *Think, Don.* The cops. Reporting Donna's absence had been his intention prior to receiving Dullington's call, but what would he say? What *could* he say?

In the time it would take for the cops to arrive, investigate the scene, and question him, he could be well on his way to meeting George Guffin at Rossetti's. Even then, Donovan knew he would be the police department's prime suspect. His wild story would be laughed at by the entire police force. They'd laugh about it for years after Donovan was locked up for murdering his wife.

He looked back at the phone. Now that calling the cops was out, Donovan was left with Dullington's demands. Aleister Dullington's explanations flew in the face of logic, but given all Donovan had seen that week, he realized he believed the man and his threats.

"The world behind the world." His stomach churned. He flickered, his office suddenly cast in a gray tone. After four days of seeing and experiencing the impossible, Donovan still found himself in disbelief. It was preposterous to believe that Donovan's boring existence could make him disappear—and yet it was happening to him at that very moment. When the flickering stopped, Donovan realized he had no choice but to accept his predicament: Dullington had him.

He thought of Donna, imagined her curled up in some dark room, the restraints cutting into her skin. What worried him wasn't her state so much as what lurked in the darkness beyond her. Though he believed Dullington's statement that no one had molested her, he was certain this was merely circumstantial, and that if he didn't act soon her situation might change.

Donovan rubbed his eyes. *Get it together. You can do this. She's okay.* Comforted by these thoughts, he picked up the phone.

"What would Joe Hopper do?"

He wouldn't call the cops, too much red tape. But who, then? The answer came immediately, blurted out by the frantic, screeching voice of his conscience: *Call the real Joe Hopper.* Michael was born to be a hero—from their childhood days in the backyard to his current career in private investigation, he always had to be the good guy. It was this trait upon which Donovan drew much of Joe Hopper's character, and one that had not diminished in its significance to Donovan despite all the intervening years of suppressed sibling rivalry.

Donovan frowned. He dialed Michael's number, his fears preparing him for assault with the press of each button. What if Michael couldn't hear him? Worse: what if he didn't believe? He hoped the news of Donna's abduction would be enough to erase any doubts his brother might have. For once, the issue at hand was not Donovan's inability to live up to his older brother's expectations.

As the phone rang a third time, Donovan realized he didn't care what Michael thought of him, so long as he got Donna back safe and sound. After a fifth ring, Michael's voicemail answered. Donovan waited for the beep, then cleared his throat. His voice sounded weak to his own ears. He cringed.

"Mike, it's Don. Listen, I need your help. I really don't know how to say this, but—aww, God, Mike, she's missing. Someone broke in and took Donna while I was at work. *Please* call me back as soon as you get this. Thanks."

He hung up the phone. The tears clouded his vision, but he did not let them keep him from moving. He made his way back downstairs.

A stiff, cool breeze greeted him with a chill as he stepped outside. He zipped up his jacket, locked the front door, and went to the car. He wiped tears from his eyes, shifted the car into reverse, and backed out of the driveway. The dashboard clock read 6:37, but he tried not to think about what he would have normally been doing on a Friday evening. Right now he had only one thing on his mind: George Guffin.

•

A jolt of pain brought Donna out of a troubled slumber. Her head swam. Everything was dark—God, the pain was horrible. Her breath was hot, and it covered her face in a thick cloud that would not diminish.

I can't breathe. The words surfaced from a murky pool of thoughts, and she panicked. She moved her head, desperate for fresh air, only the warm cloud of breath remained. She realized there was something coarse—*a cloth*—pressed against her face.

Confused, Donna tried to sit up. She wanted to pull the material from her face, only her hands would not cooperate. Something was wrong. Her heart began to race, hammering nails into her chest.

The pain in her wrists shot up into her elbows each time she tried to move, and she realized she was bound hand and foot. Memories of what happened came rushing back to her in a heap of broken images—

The man smiles and quickly shoves his weight against the door. It catches against her foot with such force that she loses her balance. The world spins, and for a moment she is falling. The floor catches her. Dazed, her head fills with sparkles of light, and she looks up to find the dirty man standing over her. She sees him reach into his pocket and pull free two items. One is a black cloth. The other is a handgun.

She panics at sight of the weapon. Her heart begins to race, and she reacts instinctively, scrambling onto her back and aiming a forceful kick at the intruder's groin. He yelps in pain and lurches over in agony. She struggles away from the door and back into the kitchen as he falls to his knees.

Donna's next impulse is to get a weapon of her own. She thinks of taking his, but realizes she hasn't the slightest idea how to use a gun, nor how to retrieve it without putting herself within his reach. He could easily grab her, wrestle her to the ground, and choke her to death. Instead she crawls to the kitchen. Her foot ignites with pain when she tries to put her weight on it, and she thinks she may have twisted it when he forced open the door.

Donna crawls to the kitchen counter. She reaches up and pulls a knife from the wooden block. She doesn't care what kind, so long as it has a blade, but before she can find one—

"You sneaky bitch."

The man is behind her. There is pain in his voice, but worse, there is anger. She feels his hands on her legs, and she cries out when he squeezes her bad ankle. Desperate, she clings to a drawer, and it gives way as he pulls her from the counter. The drawer's contents spill to the floor. She spots a steak knife and strains to reach it, but the man is one step ahead of her. He kicks it away and forces her onto her back.

He's going to rape me, she thinks. *Then he's going to kill me. A dozen images flash before her in light of this realization—things she always wanted to do, a baby she wants to have but never will, Donovan's smiling face— and regrets that she will die with him angry at her.*

Donna fights. She kicks at the man, her foot connecting with his stomach, and he yowls like an animal. Seizing the opportunity, she scrambles for the dining room, unsure of where to go but not caring so long as it's away from this lunatic. Mr. Precious Paws is underneath a chair, watching. The man mumbles something that sounds like, "I won't let you down," and he's upon her before she can climb to her feet. She rolls on her back in time to see him standing over her, a butcher knife in each hand.

He moves toward her and the cat yowls. He's stepped on Mr. Precious Paws' tail. What Donna sees next is horrifying, something that will be seared forever in her mind.

"I won't let you down," the man screams. He drops to his knees, catching the cat as it tries to escape. He holds the animal steady with one hand, brings down the knife, and exterminates Mr. Precious Paws in a single, violent stroke. Donna can see the feline's eyes, can sense its terror as the poor thing lets out a final, gurgling cry. Blood pours from its middle and its legs twitch in death throes. The knife has gone all the way through, pinning the animal to the floor.

"I. Won't. Let. You. Down."

He takes another knife and spears it through Mr. Precious Paws' neck. Blood spurts onto the wall and dribbles across the floor.

"No," Donna gasps. She cannot muster a scream. The man turns to her, shaking his head, his eyes wide with a fury she has never seen before.

"I killed the cat," he whispered, looking at the blood on his hands. He set his murderous gaze upon her. "You made me kill your fucking cat."

He pounces on her, and she does not have time to react. The man pins her to the floor. She continues to thrash, but he plants his knees on her arms. His entire weight immobilizes her. She watches his arm block out the light on the ceiling. His hand is balled into a fist, and it comes down in a swift arc.

She feels it connect with her temple, but there is no pain. There are only stars and the dark.

Donna found that darkness still lingered, and reasoned that her head was now covered by the attacker's black cloth. She tried to calm herself, holding in her breath to slow her heart. When the echo of its interminable pounding finally subsided, she discovered the sounds of movement, voices.

"Hello?" she croaked. "Somebody?"

"She's awake."

"What do we do?"

"Shut her up."

The voices were low, hushed whispers, but she could tell they belonged to men. They sounded frightened.

"Help me," she said. "I'm hurting—"

Pain shot through her right thigh. She cried out. One of the men laughed.

"Damn right, you are. Now you shut your mouth, lady, or I'll—"

"What the hell do you think you're doing?" A new voice. A woman's voice. "Get away from her."

"I don't have to take orders from you, Alice."

A loud smack echoed about the darkness. One of the men gasped. The other, Donna's attacker, fell silent.

"Maybe not," said Alice, "but I'll be god damned if I'll sit here and watch you beat her. *He* didn't tell you to do that, did he?"

There was a pause, and then the man timidly said, "No. He didn't."

"Now get out of here. *I'll* watch her." Another beat of silence filled the dark. "Go on. Fuck off, you two."

Donna chewed her bottom lip, unsure whether this Alice person was any better than the two men. And who was this "he" she referred to? Donna wondered if it was the man who abducted her.

Something pulled at the bag around her face. She gasped as its coarse surface tore away from her skin, reopening the wound she'd received with the punch that knocked her out. Dim light came into view, and she had to squint to see it. The light was orange, licking the air like a serpent's tongue. *Fire*, she thought. *It's a fire.*

A shape came into view. Donna blinked, waiting for the blurriness to subside, and she saw the face of the woman who'd come to her rescue. She was young, not yet thirty, her face spotted with dark grime. Her hair hung over her shoulders in knots.

"Here," she said. Hints of a smile teased the edges of her lips. "Drink."

She put her hand behind Donna's head, helped lift her up, and put a mug to her mouth. Donna drank the water. It was warm and bitter, but she welcomed it. When she was done, she pulled away from the mug and looked into the hardened eyes of the woman called Alice.

"Please let me go," she said. The tears returned to her eyes. "Please, I won't tell anyone. Just let me go. Let me go back to my husband."

Alice frowned. For a moment Donna feared Alice would put the bag over her head again. She watched the young woman rise to her feet, still frowning. The fire beyond the room turned Alice into a silhouette. Beyond the doorway, Donna could see columns of some kind, and benches. There were trash bags piled atop one another, a rusty shopping cart tipped on its side.

"Where are we?"

The young woman turned and shook her head.

"Just be quiet and lie still. It'll be over when he gets what he wants."

"Let me go," Donna cried. "*Please—*"

Alice left the room, pulling the door closed behind her. The darkness returned, washing over Donna's body in a quick, cold wave.

•

Traffic was light, and it did not take Donovan long to reach the diner. The parking lot was filled with Friday night patrons, and the memory of his first date here with Donna made his stomach twist into knots. He parked the car and sat for a moment.

What would he say to this man? He'd thought about it during the drive. Playing the tough guy wouldn't go over well—after all, he didn't know how closely tied this George Guffin was to Mr. Dullington. He wished his brother was home to answer his—

Phone.

Donovan remembered the cell phone. He reached into his jacket pocket and retrieved it. His heart sank. *Don't forget to charge the phone,* Donna's voice echoed in his head. The week's sudden turn off course had disrupted his usual morning routine, of which the brand new cellphone was only just becoming a part. He flipped it open. There was one bar of juice left.

He dialed his brother's number. There were three rings, followed by an error tone. He tried a second time only to be met with the same result. Donovan pulled the phone from his ear and looked at the screen: CALL FAILED.

"No shit." He looked out the window at the restaurant. "Just get it over with, Don."

His voice sounded tiny, lost. He flickered and caught a glimpse of five white figures loitering along the sidewalk. The world resumed in color. He shook off the sensation in his stomach, slid out of the car, and made his way across the parking lot. It wasn't until he reached the entrance of Rossetti's Diner that he realized he didn't know what the man looked like. He imagined a large, bulky figure—someone physically intimidating enough to force their way into his home and subdue an innocent person.

When he stepped inside, he saw no such figures. To his left and right were booths filled with teenagers, adults near his age, and even a few elderly couples. Straight ahead was a bar lined with stools and a pair of cash registers. Vintage photographs of diner promo ads from the 1950s adorned the walls, and even the wait staff were dressed in pastel colors reminiscent of the era.

Donovan stood against a sweeping tide of nostalgia. He remembered vividly the details of his and Donna's first date, the way she smiled when he opened the door for her, the scent of her perfume. The atmosphere was inviting, comforting, and made him forget about the drab alternative he'd come to know so well.

As he stood in the doorway, Donovan realized just how alone

he truly was. No one—not even the nearest waitress—looked up in his direction. *They can't see me*, he thought. The flickering overcame him, painting the café in shades of gunmetal. The diner's patrons darkened, filled in with a deep gray that obscured their features.

Except for one.

When his gray sight relented, allowing him to see the diner's vibrant shades, Donovan spotted a small man picking at a plate of greasy fries. He wore a large, green coat that seemed to swallow him. Buried underneath it were the remains of what might once have been an expensive suit. The thick-lensed glasses gave him a wide, paranoid look, his face cast in permanent shock.

The man finished his soda, cautiously eyeing Donovan's approach. He plucked two fries from his plate and stuffed them in his mouth, chewing slowly. Donovan noted the man's gaunt features, the way his face hollowed under the diner's unforgiving fluorescent lights, and the knotted strands of hair that hung over his shoulders. The sight of his Persian's dried blood staining Guffin's hands captured Donovan's attention, and he remained rooted where he stood, riding a wave of nausea.

The man's elegant posture, the way he dabbed the corners of his mouth with a napkin—these things contradicted his appearance. They weren't the manners of a soured transient.

Donovan approached the booth. "George Guffin?"

The man in the green coat nodded.

"Sit down. Candle, right?"

"That's right." Donovan took a seat across from the filthy man.

George Guffin pushed the plate of fries toward him in offering, but Donovan's attention was undistracted, staring hard into Guffin's wild eyes. He realized he was squeezing his hands into fists, and tried to relax—but how could he? This man had invaded his home and taken his wife. He wanted to be angry and violent, to smash Guffin's plate, to use its shards in torturing the truth out of him.

That's how Joe Hopper did business. The barbaric nature of his thoughts troubled Donovan. He swept them to the back of his mind.

George Guffin wiped his hands and licked his lips.

"Do you smoke?"

Donovan shook his head.

"Too bad." Guffin took a handful of fries and put them in his coat pocket. He dropped a wad of crumpled bills on the table. "Let's move this party outside, shall we?"

"Look, mister, I—"

Guffin slammed his fist on the table. "No, *you* fucking listen—" He pulled a handgun from his coat. "—Yeah, that's right. I've got your attention now, don't I?"

Donovan's blood went cold. "My undivided attention."

"Good. Now, you do what I say you do, and we'll get through this nice and quick-like. Do you understand that, Candle-man?"

Guffin tipped the barrel of the gun toward the door. Donovan left the booth with his hands held out to his sides, while Guffin followed behind. No one in the diner noticed their exit.

Donovan thought about turning on the man. He saw himself pinning Guffin to the wall and wrestling the gun from his grip.

Stay put, boss. You're no good to Donna with a hole in your head.

"Where's your car?"

"Over there." Donovan swallowed back all the nasty things he wanted to say. He calmed himself before speaking. "Mr. Guffin, I'll take you where you want to go, but just—just meet me half way, all right? Where is my wife?"

George Guffin took a deep breath and closed his eyes. "I've missed this air. So alive."

Donovan ignored him. "I asked you a question."

"And I heard you, Candle-man." Guffin opened his eyes and met Donovan's gaze. "Your wife's fine."

"That doesn't answer my question."

"I know, but I've got rules to follow, just like you do." Guffin frowned. "Now I suggest you take me where I need to go."

A young couple walked past them toward the diner. They ignored the weapon in Guffin's hand. The world went gray for a moment, and Donovan saw the white creatures on their shoulders. When he looked back at Guffin, he could tell that he, too, saw the little abominations.

"You can see them?"

The world flickered back into color. Guffin nodded. "Of

course I can see them. Dullington gave me a free pass tonight to do what I need to do, and—" His face flushed. He jammed the gun barrel into Donovan's gut. "Quit stalling."

Free pass? Donovan filed it away for later. He did as he was told, and led Guffin to his car. They got in, and Donovan asked their destination as he started engine.

"You know the parking garage at 8th and Dwyer?"

Donovan thought for a moment and nodded.

"Other side of town, across from the courthouse?"

"You got it, Candle-man. And no funny stuff—or I'll blow your fucking head off."

•

It took them a while to reach the garage. Friday night traffic was slow-moving as they crossed into the city, making Donovan even more tense. When they turned onto Dwyer Street, Guffin leaned forward in his seat and placed the handgun on the dash. Donovan caught a glimpse of it and wondered if it was real. He decided he did not want to find out.

"Three more blocks. It's on your left."

"Mr. Guffin," Donovan said, "are you going to tell me what this is about? I mean, really?"

"You know what it's about."

Donovan stopped at a red light, taking the opportunity to look over at his captor. "I know what's happening to me, but I don't understand it."

"Trust me, Candle-man, you don't want to."

"You understand it?"

"I understand you need to shut your fucking mouth." Guffin took hold of the handgun. "This is about what *he* wants, and I should know. I've seen others play his games. This was my turn. We're all his puppets. He makes the rules, and we move to his whim."

"We?"

Guffin did not reply. The light turned green, and they sped through the intersection. The garage at the corner of 8th and Dwyer covered more than half a city block. From the street, it bore the appearance of a fortress. Donovan guided the sedan into the entrance and pulled a ticket from the gate. The crossbar rose, and he tapped the gas.

"Top floor, Candle-man."

They ascended slowly. Guffin did not object to their speed. Donovan took the opportunity to scout the surrounding levels in hopes that someone—anyone—might be parked there for the evening. To his dismay, the garage was empty except for a few cars on the bottom two levels. He parked alongside the edge of the roof overlooking the entrance.

When he turned off the engine, Guffin raised the gun and shook his head.

"Leave the keys."

Donovan slowly raised his hands. He tried to keep himself from shaking, but his body refused to obey. "Okay," he whispered. "No keys."

"Get out, Candle-man."

Donovan did so. Clouds rolled overhead, and thunder clapped in the distance. From this height he could see the twinkling lights of the lower city, as well as some of the taller skyscrapers. Across the street, the courthouse shone bright with orange halogen lights, illuminating the statue in the courtyard. Donovan cracked a smile, remembering a time when he and some college friends toilet-papered the old statue while Donna and the rest of their girlfriends watched with feigned amusement.

That memory stirred the chunk of ice in Donovan's stomach, and he turned to face Guffin. The car separated them, and it was for the best. Donovan wanted to tear him in half.

"Where is she?" he asked.

"Who? Your wife?"

"*Where is she?*" Donovan half-screamed, half-growled. He took a step around the car. Guffin raised the gun.

"You stay right there, Candle-man. Hands on your head."

Donovan stopped in his tracks, doing as he was told. A cold breeze rose up around them. Lightning flashed, followed closely by a crash of thunder. He felt a few drops of rain on his head and hands.

"What are you getting out of this?"

Under the glare of the garage lights, he could see the man's hands shaking. Guffin approached him. He wore a frown, and his eyes appeared so wide through his thick glasses that Donovan feared they might pop from his skull. Droplets of rain rolled off his coat.

Donovan glanced at his feet, measuring the space between himself and his captor. *Two steps*, he thought. *Maybe three.* His heart thudded a cacophonous rhythm in his ribcage. Was he really going to do this? Could he? He thought of Donna tied up somewhere at the mercy of a lunatic, and decided he would damn well try.

"Answer my question, Guffin."

"A permanent free pass. He lets me out of his hell. I do this, and he'll let me go. That's the plan. That's our agreement. I bring you here, he takes you, and I stay. Goddamnit, that's how it's supposed to go. *Where are you, Dullington?*"

Guffin trembled as he screeched into the wind. He lowered the gun, and Donovan made his move. His hands took on a life of their own, moving against his better judgment, and they connected with the muzzle. Startled, Guffin jerked his hand away, but in his haste, he lost his grip. The gun hit the ground and went off, startling both of them.

Donovan met the eyes of his adversary. In that moment he saw only Donna, her hands bound, a bag over her head. He saw the terrified, lifeless eyes of Mr. Precious Paws.

Get 'em, boss.

He charged forward and tackled George Guffin. The collision sent both sprawling to the ground. Donovan's hands found their way to Guffin's throat.

"You bastard, yo—*urch.*"

Donovan squeezed as hard as he could, concentrating the pressure of his fingers into the tender flesh of Guffin's neck. He was so intent on crushing the man's trachea that he didn't see Guffin's free hand until it was too late. Guffin's fist cracked against Donovan's jaw. An assortment of colored lights exploded before his eyes, followed by a searing, white pain. The force flung him back onto the cold concrete. He tried to shake off the splotches of purple and black.

Guffin climbed to his feet. He hacked and coughed, rubbing at his throat.

"You motherfuckin' asshole." He stumbled, regained his footing, and planted a swift kick into Donovan's ribs. The blow cleared all the misshapen forms from Donovan's eyes, and he managed to catch Guffin's foot before he could land a second kick. In an act of desperation, he sank his teeth into Guffin's ankle. He clamped his jaw down as hard and as far as it would go, tearing through the man's flesh and stopping only when he reached bone. The coppery taste of blood filled his mouth but he dared not stop—not now.

This is for Donna, he thought, and bit down even harder.

Guffin uttered a scream rivaled only by the thunderclap overhead. He fell backward, kicking his foot free of Donovan's mouth. A chunk of flesh came away with it. When Donovan realized he still held a piece of Guffin between his teeth, he spat it out and retched. Guffin cried in agony as he scrambled to put pressure on the wound.

Lightning split the sky, followed by another heavy crash of thunder. Sheets of rain fell down upon them. It made seeing difficult, but Donovan found what he was looking for in the pale light. The gun lay just beside the car's rear tire. He crawled across the pavement and claimed it; he turned, braced himself against the back of the car, and watched Guffin writhe in pain.

"You . . . you *bit* me."

Donovan blinked. "You kidnapped my wife."

He climbed to his feet, wincing at the sharp pain stabbing into his ribs, and approached his wife's assailant, aiming the gun at Guffin's head.

"Start talking, Mr. Guffin."

Blood gushed from the wound in his ankle, forming a dark pool around his leg. Supine and vulnerable, Guffin was far smaller than Donovan first realized. Buried within the bulk of the coat and draped in the remains of a suit was a small-framed man suffering from weeks, if not months of starvation. As the rain fell down upon them, Donovan Candle felt pity for him.

"Fuck you, Candle-man." Guffin spat.

Donovan squeezed the trigger. The recoil sent the bullet off course, barely missing Guffin's head. It startled Donovan so badly that he almost dropped the gun.

"He played me," Guffin groaned. "He'll play you, too. Dullington's sadistic. He's using us, feeding on us."

Feeding on us. Donovan shivered.

"There are others like you 'n me. He lets us out sometimes, only lets people see us when he wants them to. Some forget about us and others don't. We're just his pupp—" Guffin's eyes grew wide. He screamed. "Oh God, please no, not now—"

At first Donovan did not understand what was happening, or to whom Guffin was speaking. The hiss of rain became muffled, and when he blinked, he found himself in the midst of the gray sight. Sensations of rain and damp air were displaced by an unsettling emptiness; the sprawling cityscape was but a lifeless outline on the horizon.

Donovan blinked a second time, and the gray sight still remained. He looked down just in time to watch his body flicker and solidify.

George Guffin moaned. Donovan looked up and saw the man flickering as well. The pool of blood around his ankle now appeared as a black puddle.

"—no, please no, please, *please! What did I do wrong?*"

A low, mournful sob came from behind. Donovan turned, and watched in frightened awe as one of the albino figures approached. His whole body went cold. The world was soundless but for his heart, pounding with a fury all its own.

"Not the Yawning! *ALEISTER! PLEASE!*"

As the albino thing neared, Donovan realized just how large it actually was: seven, maybe even eight feet tall. Its hulking arms stretched down to the ground, dragging lazily behind as it took one determined step after another. It paused for a moment, regarding Donovan with its empty eyes, then uttered a low sound that could only be described as Guffin had in his shriek mere moments before.

Yawning.

Guffin beckoned to Donovan. "Help me! Candle-man, I-I'm sorry, just—*fuck, just* HELP ME! HELP M—"

The Yawning stood over Guffin and leered, swaying to and fro on its spindly legs. Its mouth shivered and twitched. Donovan could only watch, frozen in place by his terror. The Yawning's mouth trembled a moment longer, then opened. Wide, wider still, it formed an elongated, gaping maw that appeared to be bottomless.

And still its mouth opened, stretching until its jaw hit the ground.

Guffin screamed. *"NO! ALEISTER, I'M SORRY! I'M SO SORR—"* The otherwise sluggish creature moved with sudden, ravenous speed, engulfing the screeching man into its blackened hole of a mouth. A sickening crunch of bone issued from the monster as its jaw closed, rejoining its head.

Donovan gasped, felt his stomach lurch. "Oh Christ."

The albino thing turned and faced him. A dark, red ring circled its thin lips. George Guffin was no more.

Now it was only Donovan and the Yawning.

-6-
MONOCHROME

The Yawning towered over him, its giant, pale knuckles scraping the ground in slow arcs. It put Donovan in mind of the lummox often portrayed in the cartoons of his youth. Had it not been for the horror he'd just witnessed, he would have suspected the giant to be as playful as a dimwitted Labrador. The albino thing lurched forward, raised its elongated arm, and beckoned to him. Its quivering jaw relaxed as its mouth opened, and from it came that same low-pitched howl. It echoed in the empty air and carried across the gray, lifeless cityscape, inciting answers to its solitary call from other Yawning somewhere below.

The sound sent chills racing down his body, snapping him from his frozen state and urging his feet to move. On the far side of the rooftop, just beyond the creature, was an access door to the garage stairwell. The Yawning took a long stride toward him, and Donovan reacted without thought, bolting for the door. He charged forward, past the hulking beast, feeling its coarse flesh scrape his arm as he went by. The almost sticky sensation reminded him of rubber.

His mind raced. *This isn't happening. This can't be happening. He—it just gobbled him up.*

Donovan kept running. He knew that if he stopped, he would scrutinize and postulate, and now wasn't the time. The last thing he wanted was to be consumed like the unfortunate George Guffin.

His footsteps marked muffled thuds across the darkened pavement. His previous exposures to the gray sight had been limited to glimpses of what lay beyond the world's veil. Now, as he raced across the garage rooftop, Donovan realized just how empty everything actually was. He could see the faint droplets of rain falling all around him, but he could not feel their touch on his body. There was no breeze as he ran, no violent storm gusts, and the crash of thunder that should be overhead was absent. Lightning in this realm flashed a more brilliant shade of white, blanketing the landscape for an instant.

Donovan did not dare to stop and ponder the gray world's intricacies. Instead, he ran as fast and as hard as his body allowed. His chest heaved, lungs ablaze with a fire that urged him forward. Every breath was combustion.

He looked back only once, and that was all the motivation he needed: the Yawning lumbered after him. Despite its sluggish pace, its long, scrawny legs carried it a great distance with each stride. When Donovan reached the door, the albino monstrosity was perhaps 300 feet away, a gap which narrowed with each lumbering step.

Donovan stumbled down the stairs, shoes slapping loudly against concrete in the empty space. He cleared the last four steps with a single leap, pausing long enough to get his bearings. The door opened above, and that long, guttural sob followed soon after, filling the stairwell with a vicious melancholy that horrified him.

He looked up. The Yawning glared down at him and uttered another moan.

"Damn." He willed his legs to move again. They carried him out the door and into the street, where he expected to see two lanes full of gray, dull cars. To his surprise, there were none.

For the first time since the transition, Donovan saw the Monochrome in full clarity. It was an image of the regular world. bled of color and wiped of all texture. In this guise, the city at ground level appeared as a series of jutting structures composed of complex, planar geometry.

Another moan echoed from down the street. The second Yawning rounded the corner of what once was the courthouse. More appeared from behind an object Donovan recognized as the courthouse statue. Further on down the street, he saw three more emerge from another structure's entrance.

He realized then, with heart-sinking certainty, that he might outrun them now, but his legs would give out sooner or later.

A door slammed open from behind. He turned just as the first Yawning shouldered itself through the opening.

He sprinted away from the garage and the courthouse, diverging from the path he and Guffin had taken to get there. It wasn't until he'd crossed over a bridge that he realized he had not a clue as to his whereabouts. Without definition, all the city's buildings looked the same, and Donovan had no reliable landmarks. The Yawning, for all he knew, were still hot on his trail, but hopefully he'd bought himself enough time to pause and think.

Okay. You can do this. For Donna. Think, Don. North side of the city. Courthouse, garage—

He turned back and faced the direction from which he'd come, tracing a mental map from where he was to the direction he hoped would lead back to the highway. The highway itself, he realized, probably wasn't a great idea, though. He remembered his commutes earlier that week, during which the random bouts of gray sight revealed hundreds of the lurking, white monstrosities standing between rows of traffic.

If one spotted him, it would call out to its friends, and he'd soon have an entire population of them breathing down his neck.

George Guffin's screaming face flashed before his eyes, and Donovan shook his head in disgust. For the first time since his flight from the garage, Donovan noticed he still held the man's gun. He wondered if a bullet could take down one of those freaks, if a bullet would even be useful in this reality. Then he laughed at himself, a dry stuttering wheeze. He'd never fired a gun before tonight, and that had been an accident. All he had to go by was what he'd seen in movies. His brother was the real gun expert—

Michael Candle's face popped into his head. He turned in the opposite direction, gambling that the street to his back was Poplar.

If his mental compass was accurate, this street would take him right to Michael's neighborhood. It seemed as good a destination as any other. Getting back to the real world was a mystery he'd have to solve when he arrived. Walking to his own home would take hours, and there was no telling how many of those things stalked the monochromatic streets.

Get moving, boss.

Donovan jogged toward the street corner and froze when he heard the sob of a nearby Yawning. It turned the corner ahead of him and stopped alongside the adjacent building. It swayed, its jaw quivering, peering at him with two beady, black eyes.

Silence moved into the gap between them, broken only by the rapid thump-thump-thump of Donovan's pounding heart. It sounded like a marching band warming up in his head. He wondered if the creature could hear it too.

The Yawning steadied its face and opened its mouth. Donovan feared what might come next. If it made a sound, the entire area would know he was there. He had only a moment to react, and in that precise instant, he decided he couldn't risk another Yawning alarm.

He raised the gun and fired. The shot jarred him, filling his ears with a low ring. When his senses cleared, he saw the Yawning still stood. It held one clumsy hand to its chest, examining a wound that did not bleed. It looked over at Donovan, opened its mouth, and vented a deep, horrific growl. It was the sound of metal scraped against a chalkboard, inciting chills across the back of Donovan's neck.

Good job, Don. He was already running when the white thing took its first steps toward him. His legs felt like rubber as they carried him through an intersection he thought to be Poplar and Rose. There he paused just long enough to look back and watch the Yawning bellow one of its angry, communicative calls. A chorus of responses rose from deep within the labyrinthine city, heightening his terror and urging him to move. *Don't stop*, his conscience told him, *don't look back, just go! Go, go!*

When he turned the corner, he found himself on another unfamiliar street. He cursed himself for staying away from the inner city for so many years. It was then he caught sight of the row of gray trees.

The city park. He raced ahead, feet clattering across the pavement. The Yawning echoed from behind, but all he could hear was the frantic pacing of his heart.

•

Donovan found his bearings among the grove of trees. From there, he supposed, it would be only an hour before he reached Michael's house. What he would do once he got there was a mystery to him, but he tried not to think about it.

The park covered most of a city block, making it almost impossible to get lost among the trees and pathways. In the Monochrome, however, everything was a mere shade lighter or darker than everything else. Donovan struggled with a landscape in which even the trees lacked distinction. Viewed against a backdrop of gray forms, the sameness was disorienting. It wasn't until he found the fountain that he discovered his place within the grove. He leaned against a nearby tree, caught his breath, and stared at the fountain's rim.

He and Donna had spent their third date here huddled on the grass, watching the water spout up in the fountain's center.

It was Homecoming night, and most of their friends were in the stands, cheering for the football team as they clashed against their long-time rivals. The choice to visit the park was happenstance. Neither of them cared for sports, the movies were sold out, and they'd just left a small restaurant a few, short blocks away. They walked hand in hand. It was a clear night, and despite the crowds gathered for Homecoming, it was mostly silent. He remembered Donna's concerns as they strolled through the park. She worried they would be mugged, or worse. He'd assured her that he would protect her no matter what.

No one troubled them that night. They sat together and watched as life moved on around them.

Donna put her head on his shoulder.

"I think I love you, Donnie Candle."

He rested his head against hers and took her hand, threading their fingers together.

"I think you do," he whispered. "That's okay, because I think I love you, too."

Donovan resisted the tears elicited by the tender memory. He pushed away from the tree and passed the fountain, following a walkway to the park's plaza. A pair of vendor shacks, once decorated with menus and graffiti, stood out like two gray monoliths. He stopped beside the nearest one and rubbed his eyes.

How could he let this happen? He'd been careless with his own life, and now Donna might have to pay for it. He regretted not conceding to her wishes Monday night. All she wanted was to get away for the weekend. She was right—it wouldn't break their bank account. He knew that. Even a full week away wouldn't do them in. Years ago he would've agreed to it without a moment's hesitation.

Donovan shivered. When had he grown so selfish and boring? Perhaps Aleister Dullington was right. He *was* saturated with mediocrity.

Chin up, boss. This ain't over yet.

It wasn't. Donovan took a breath, making a silent vow to take Donna on a real vacation when they made it through this, whatever *this* was.

"Okay," he said. His voice sounded tiny amidst the silence of the world. "Get a grip on yourself, Don. Keep moving. Kee—"

Movement stole his attention. It was nearby, a subtle scuttling putting him in mind of a seething multitude of insects.

Donovan raised the gun and peered around the corner of the shack toward the grove of trees. What he saw made a pit open in his stomach and all his insides fall into his feet.

The tiny, white things marched across the grass, a veritable army of them numbering in the thousands. They looked harmless while standing on the shoulders of others; now, as they advanced, he found their mass intimidating. There was more movement in his peripheral vision. A small wave of the little bastards crashed over the fountain, their pudgy bodies sprawling across the walkway. Their backward voices meshed into a constant, buzzing drone as they advanced.

He looked at the 9mm, then back at the swarming, white legion.

One of the things saw him. It screeched and pointed. The others cheered.

"I'm not seeing this." His declaration fell deaf against their wall of reversed language. He tried to look away, but found he couldn't take his eyes off them.

The throng of miniature albino soldiers marched onward. When they reached the plaza's perimeter, Donovan turned and ran, managing only a few strides before he realized he was surrounded. The Lilliputian monsters streamed from all corners, over the grass, the benches, even on the limbs of trees. He was lost in the Monochrome wilderness, and had stumbled into a hive.

Donovan stepped back against the wall of the shack and raised the pistol. *I'm going to die here*, he thought. *They're going to drag me down and tear me to pieces.*

The creatures stopped a few feet away. They chattered in unison, looking up at him from a sea of black, empty eyes.

"It is a shame Mr. Guffin could not follow instructions."

The creatures fell silent as Aleister Dullington's voice boomed overhead. Donovan felt the ground vibrate with each pronounced syllable. On the phone, Dullington was soft spoken, disarming. In the Monochrome, his voice thundered with authority, asserting one immutable fact: this was his kingdom, and here he was God.

Donovan turned, frantically searching for his enemy, but the voice came from everywhere. A mound rose in the center of the white swarm as the creatures piled upon one another, writhing like maggots on a corpse. When one climbed up to join the mass, a new feature sprouted from the whole. Extensions took shape as limbs; a stump became a hand, fingers seemingly carved out of the air by an unseen knife. The figure of a man slowly took shape out of the squirming mass. Two arms connected to a torso, the torso to a head, and the black eyes of the white creatures came together, forming a pair of bulbous, obsidian orbs.

The white flesh dimmed, outlining the features of a robe. Aleister Dullington stepped out of the pale mass, walking atop their writhing bodies as if on water. His ashen robe draped from his shoulders to the mass of creatures below, and Donovan could not tell where one ended and the other began.

They're a part of him, Donovan realized. *And he's a part of them. He sees what they see.* Suddenly everything he knew of the creatures made sense. They were Dullington's sentinels, their language his own.

Aleister Dullington's features were pale, sallow. The man had no eyelids, eyebrows, or any hair on his head. At a glance, Dullington looked like an adult with the oversized head of a newborn.

"My sincerest apologies, Mr. Candle. I did not instruct him to murder your cat. Perhaps I waited too long to give Mr. Guffin his opportunity; he was overzealous."

Dullington approached him. Donovan discovered he was too frightened to move.

"I must say, you continue to surprise me, Mr. Candle. The way you handled him was most unexpected. You are proving to be quite entertaining. I am glad I chose you." The creatures beneath his feet chortled together. Dullington looked down at them, listening. He smiled. His teeth were broken, jagged. "The Cretins say you have spirit. I am apt to agree."

Donovan looked down at the army of creatures. They snickered in unison.

"Where's my wife?" He hated how frail he sounded.

"In due time, Mr. Candle."

"No," Donovan said, raising his voice. "You fucking tell me where she is or I'll blow your head off."

He pointed the gun at Dullington's bulbous head. The man made no expression. His empty, black eyes peered into Donovan.

"You cannot kill me, Mr. Candle. Your bullets mean nothing here, nor do your empty threats. Do not misunderstand your position."

Donovan slowly lowered his weapon. "Guffin said you played him. How do I know you won't do the same to me?"

"Mr. Guffin did not play by the rules I set."

"What rules?"

"Simple rules, Mr. Candle. I gave him the opportunity—much like I am giving you an opportunity—to redeem himself by doing what I myself cannot. I told him to take your wife without doing harm. I did not tell him to take a life as well."

"What was his reward?"

A corner of Dullington's upper lip twitched. "Respite from this place."

"Would you have let him go?" Donovan watched his enemy bow his head in thought. He realized the man looked like a demonic monk.

"I would. There will always be others." A thin smile spread across his pallid face. "Always people like you."

Chills crept down Donovan's spine. *People like you.* His mouth was suddenly very dry.

"You are my puppet, Mr. Candle. Make no mistake of that. I am using you, just as I used Guffin, and just as I have used countless others."

Donovan remembered their conversation earlier that day. "This person you want me to find, is he one of your puppets, too?"

Aleister Dullington frowned. For a moment Donovan feared he'd touched a nerve, but the hints of emotion on his adversary's face were short-lived.

"I believe 'puppet' is too harsh a term. *Protégé* would be the correct nomenclature, but that is not for discussion at this time, Mr. Candle." His face lightened. "Tonight was a test to see if you truly are the right man for the job. You performed well, and as a reward, I will allow you to speak with your wife."

He reached into his robe and pulled out a small, black cell phone.

"Consider this a down payment in good faith."

Speak with your wife. The prospect made Donovan's heart sing. Finally, to hear her voice! Dullington stepped forward, offering him the phone. It had no buttons, no antenna—instead it merely contained a speaker and mouthpiece. He reached for it, but Dullington snatched it away at the last moment.

"You will return to your reality when you are finished."

Donovan eyed the phone, ravenous with the thought of hearing Donna's voice.

"And then what?"

"And then you will await further instructions. My Cretins will not inhibit your progress, so do not fear speaking to your brother. He will see you."

This startled Donovan. He didn't want to show it, but when he looked into Dullington's empty eyes, he realized there was nothing he could hide.

"Call your wife."

Dullington held out the phone. Donovan hesitated a moment

before taking it. He put it to his ear, recoiling from a sharp hiss of electronic interference. It was brief, fading into the low chirp of a soft ringing. A click followed.

There were voices of men and women in the background. He heard someone say "Speak."

"D-Donna?"

Heavy breathing filled the line, inhaling and exhaling in quick gasps.

"Don? Donnie, is that you?"

"Honey, God, oh God, baby are you okay? Has he hurt you?"

"My head hurts, but I'm all right. Where are you, Don?"

The sound of suppressed sobs in her throat forced tears from his eyes. Words escaped him. Where *was* he?

"I-I'm in the city, near the park. Our place in the park. Listen, I can't talk for long, honey. I'm coming for you. I promise, I—"

"I love you so much, Donovan, I lov—"

The line went dead, and Dullington plucked the phone from his ear. He was still forming the words to reciprocate his love when he met Aleister's lidless gaze. He forced himself to stare deep into those glassy, black orbs with a newfound ferocity.

"That is enough for now, Mr. Candle. You will return to the Spectrum. Expect to hear from me on the morrow."

Aleister Dullington offered Donovan a stoic nod. The Cretins chortled in their backward voices, providing a unified laugh track. Their laughter grew dim as the flickering overtook him, their bodies fading out of existence as the world came to life. Texture and color returned, as did the steady rainfall once again pelting his head.

Donovan found himself alone in the city park. He blinked a few times, trying to accommodate the onslaught of color and depth. Friday night sounds met his ears. Crowds of people huddled beneath umbrellas rushed by on the sidewalk ahead of him. Cars honked and came to a full stop as traffic lights changed.

His body tingled for a moment as the flickering swept over him, and then it was gone.

He took a deep breath. The cold air was refreshing, not stale like that of the Monochrome. What had Dullington called this side of reality? The Spectrum? *Fitting*, he thought, then remembered his original goal: he had to get to his brother's house.

Donovan tucked Guffin's pistol into the back of his pants. He turned, surveying the park to get his bearings. Another breeze swept over him, chilling him to his core. He zipped up his jacket, shoved his hands in his pockets, and began the walk back to his car. Along the way, he tried to work out the situation with Aleister Dullington and this mystery man he was supposed to find, but most of all it was Donna who dominated his thoughts. She was out there, somewhere, scared and waiting for him to come to her rescue.

He forged into the downpour, his wife at the forefront of his mind. It was her image that kept him warm in the cold night air.

I'm coming, honey. I'll find you. I promise.

-7-
THE MISSING

ONE MOMENT HER husband was there, a panicked voice out of the dark, and then he was gone again. Donna tried not to cry.

The haggard, young thing in the tattered clothes pulled the phone from Donna's ear and frowned. She gave off a stench that curdled Donna's stomach, as though she hadn't bathed in months. Judging by what little she'd seen of the woman, Donna suspected this was not far from the truth.

The flames of a barrel burning just beyond the doorway licked the air, casting wicked shadows over the area. The heat stung her eyes, and she had to look away. The young woman sat beside her for a moment, staring at the floor.

"Alice? That's your name, isn't it?"

She looked down at Donna and slowly nodded. Even in the dim light, Donna could see the life in this woman's eyes.

"Please talk to me."

"I'm not supposed to."

"Can you tell me where my husband is?"

Alice looked away. "He's in the Monochrome."

Donna opened her mouth to inquire, but stopped short when

Alice produced a roll of duct tape. She tore off a small strip.

"Sweetheart, you don't have to do that. I'll be quiet if that's what you need me to do."

Alice paused. She stared hard at Donna, gauging whether or not she was serious.

"Not a word?"

"Not a word. Cross my heart." Donna offered a smile, and she thought she saw the faint traces of one reciprocated on Alice's face, but the light was too dim to know for sure. She shifted her weight and leaned down next to Donna's ear.

"You're a nice lady, and I want to see you through this. If anyone comes near you, you scream, okay? You scream, and I'll come running. Not all of us are good. Some of us deserve to be here."

Her words made Donna's heart race, and she tried to ignore the stench of Alice's breath. *You scream. Not all of us are good.*

Alice stood up and backed out of the room. She put a finger to her lips as she closed the door. Darkness filled the enclosure, punctuated by a sliver of flickering light that seeped through a crack beneath the door. Voices came from beyond her prison, but she couldn't make them out. As before, she was alone with nothing but her own thoughts.

She winced as she forced herself onto her side, wiggling her fingers and toes to keep the blood flowing. Her head still ached from the blow. She feared she might have a concussion, but tried to keep her mind off the pain. It wasn't easy.

Donna thought of her husband, trying to picture his face and wondering where he was at the moment. He'd said he was at their place in the park. It made little sense as to why he was there, but given all that had happened, not much else made sense, either. There was someone else with him, though she did not hear his voice. She'd heard the others outside her cell mention a name—Dullington— and the fear in their voices told her one thing: he was the one behind all this. They feared him, and it was so great a fear that they did whatever he told them to.

Who he was, and why he was doing all of this, was beyond her. She could think of nothing she and Donovan had done to offend anyone. They weren't rich, so that left out ransom as a motive. What, then? Donna sighed, thinking back to the phone call. Donovan seemed rushed, distracted by something else. And he sounded so far away.

She tried not to think about that. Hearing his voice in this murky place was dream-like. It was the last thing she expected would happen, but when she saw the phone in Alice's hand, her heart leapt up with the hope that it would be her love on the other side. There was something in his voice, though. It was something that had been there for the past week, something she couldn't put her finger on.

"Distant" came to mind, and she realized that was a perfect way to describe his behavior. There were times when she felt he wasn't there at all, as if he was just a ghost haunting their home as she went about her day. Sometimes she'd hear him speak, only to look up and find she was alone in the room. And the headaches—God, the headaches were unbearable.

It was stress. Had to be. Donovan's stress became her stress, and that gave her the migraines. And his stress was that job. Always, *that job*. She knew it wasn't good for him. He was meant for something more than that, but—

His voice spoke up in her head before she could finish the thought: *But we needed the money*. That disturbed her. Fresh out of college, they had their share of debts. He'd graduated a year ahead of her; she, in the midst of finding her way, opted to take a year away from collegiate life in order to figure out what she wanted to do. "The real world" stepped in, and chose for her.

With the economy in piss-poor shape, Donovan had few opportunities for steady employment. It was either fast food or Identinel. There weren't many jobs available for a liberal arts major. He'd applied to Identinel under the pretense that it would be a stepping stone to something better. She'd taken various part-time jobs, but in the end, responsibility fell to her husband to bring home the bread.

Things got better over the years—they were certainly better off now—and she found that she loved and respected him even more with each passing day. But there was still that job.

Donna twiddled her fingers to keep the blood flowing. Ghostly pins prickled her fingertips.

Identinel turned out to be just as she'd feared. It was fine those first few years, but as they started to pile on more responsibilities, Donovan grew more and more detached. He allowed them to mold him into what they wanted him to be: a company man.

She dry-swallowed and listened to her throat click. Identinel consumed him. They led him along with a carrot on a string, promising more and more, but in the end it never amounted to as much as they took away. He was stuck there, she realized, and the company knew it.

Donna realized she had to pee. She wanted to call out, tell them she had to go to the bathroom, but remembered her promise to Alice. The thought of duct tape wrapped around her mouth didn't seem pleasant.

She squeezed her thighs together to hold back the sudden ache in her bladder.

He'll come, she thought. *He'll get us out of this mess.* And when he did, she'd embrace him, shower him with kisses, make love to him until exhaustion overtook them both. She wanted so badly to apologize for their argument Monday night. She feared that, somehow, it was the start of all this. Everything seemed fine before then.

That's not true, spoke her conscience. *It was just the last straw. Things weren't fine. You weren't happy.*

It was true. She was unhappy—not with him, but with the way his job had ruined his life. She saw him slaving over his writing, watched him put it off to work overtime at the office. In college, he lived for his writing. He had big dreams. He wanted to be the next Raymond Chandler. Observing him slowly walk away from that dream, when it had defined him for years beforehand, depressed her. She wanted the best for her husband, and she wanted him to be happy.

Identinel had afforded them a means to live, but not much else. If they came out of this in one piece, she would make him quit that horrid job.

But what about the baby? she heard him ask. If they wanted a baby, they had to save and save and save—

What about living? she wondered. They'd barely lived their own lives—what made them think they could foster another life into being?

Stop it. Just stop it. Keep it together, or there will be no baby.

Donna blinked away tears.

You'll see him again. He's going to figure this out. He always finds a way.

The ache in her bladder prompted a round of shivers. She tried to squeeze her legs tighter, but in the end, she gave up the fight. Warm urine gushed, then trickled between her legs, soaking her clothes, and forming a puddle around her waist. The heat of shame overcame her, and she reminded herself that it didn't matter anymore.

She shivered, yearning for freedom from her dark prison. Her head swam, and she closed her eyes, eager to be rid of the chills and the frustration and the loss. Before she found sleep, Donna had one silent, troubling thought:

Oh Don, where are you?

•

"Was that good for you?"

She rolled off him, perching herself on the edge of the bed in a single, fluid motion. He was impressed, but figured she'd had plenty of opportunities to perfect her craft. *Maybe,* he thought, *or maybe she's just a good actress.*

Albert Sparrow sat up against the headboard. He reached over and flipped on the hotel lamp.

"It certainly was."

The prostitute looked over her shoulder. The way her black hair spilled down her naked back roused his interest. Maybe he'd have another go with her before sending her on her way.

Her coquettish smile was infectious. He leered at her, grinning ear to ear. He was old enough to be her father.

"So, my dear—" He climbed out of bed and walked across the suite. He put on a white robe.

"—how, exactly, does one become a woman of your *profession?*"

She looked away, embarrassed.

"Forgive me," he said. "Drink?" Sparrow gestured to the mini-bar.

The woman—he thought her name was Lindsay—offered a sheepish smile and nodded. Sparrow smiled again. He opened the door, plucked two single-serving bottles of whiskey from the top shelf, and poured them into a pair of tumblers.

She grinned when he handed her the glass, and drank its contents in one gulp. "Thanks, mister—"

"*Doctor.*"

"Oh." Lindsay—or was it Linda?—brushed the hair from her eyes. Sparrow pulled his own silvery hair back into a ponytail. "What sort of doctor?"

"The scholarly kind. *Philosophiae doctor.*" He made a theatrical bow. "Dr. Albert Sparrow, at your service."

"Wow. Aren't you the author of that book—" She snapped her fingers, searching for the title. "A Life—something."

"*A Life Ordinary: A Comprehensive Study in Human Mediocrity.*"

"That's the one!" she giggled. "I heard you on the radio."

"Indeed."

He strolled over to the dresser and slowly opened the top drawer. He saw what he was looking for, smiled, and put his hand on it.

"Tell me, Lindsay—"

"Lanna."

"Apologies, *Lanna*. What did you want to do in life? Surely this wasn't it."

Her face darkened, cheeks flushing a deep red. Lanna looked toward the window with its drawn curtains, then back toward the door. Sparrow stood between her and the exit.

"Lanna?"

"Huh? Oh—a dancer. I wanted to be a dancer, but—I dropped out of school because I needed the money, yeah, and then I fell on bad times, my mother got sick and I had to help her out, so—"

Sparrow let his smile fall. He stared hard at the woman, right in the eye, so she would know he *knew*.

"—I think I should be going." Lanna lunged for her purse. Sparrow lifted the gun from the drawer, pointed it at her pretty face. She froze in mid-step.

"The first thing I learned about lying was to keep it simple. Never embellish more than you have to." He motioned to the bed. "Have a seat. You're going to tell me everything."

Lanna glanced back at her purse. It didn't match her thousand-dollar price tag. It was stained, dirty, like she'd found it at the bottom of a dumpster. Sparrow closed the gap between them and pressed the gun barrel against her forehead.

"Sit down."

She did as he bade her. Sparrow took a step back, lowered his weapon, and looked over at her handbag. He went through its contents: a revolver, a couple of spare bullets, a pack of smokes, a lighter, and a photograph. Sparrow smirked, held up the photo and showed it to her.

"Do you think the photographer got my best side?" Lanna turned away, her head down like a scolded child. Sparrow looked at the photo. "I still can't believe they picked this one for the book jacket. Such a shame." He shook his head.

"Look, mister—"

"Doctor."

"*Dr.* Sparrow—we don't have to do this. He just wanted me to find you, and—"

He lifted the handgun from her purse. "Coerce me? Allow me a moment, dear, and tell you what *I* know. *I* know you aren't the first. *I* know you won't be the last. He's had Missing just like you on my trail since the day I escaped, and I've got news for you, missy—"

Sparrow thrust himself upon her. She tried to scream, but he was too fast for her. His hands found her throat. Lanna slapped his head, his shoulders, trying to beat him back, but Sparrow would not be denied his freedom. He dug his fingers into her flesh, grimacing like a rabid dog as he watched the life drain from her eyes.

"I'm not going back. Not for him, *never in a million—fucking—years*—and *certainly* not because of a pretend-whore like you."

Spittle flew from his lips, splattering against her cheek, but Lanna did not notice. She stared up at him, her eyes affixed to his. He heard her last breath leave her, a hushed, death-whimper that almost made him feel pity.

Almost.

He gave her throat one more squeeze to be sure. She did not move.

Dr. Sparrow climbed off her body, wiped the sweat from his forehead and spittle from his chin. He stepped away from the bed. The room flickered for a moment, as did Lanna's body.

"Take her back," he whispered. "Go on, take her back. Get rid of the evidence for me."

He'd seen it happen many times before. The first time he witnessed it, it scared the hell out of him. That was years ago, and it got much easier each time.

Lanna's body dimmed, flickered, and vanished from the bed. An imprint of her body remained in the sheets. *Once a part of the Monochrome, always a part of the Monochrome.* Dullington didn't let go unless he chose to.

Sparrow opened the mini-bar and took out a tiny bottle of vodka. He unscrewed the cap and drank it in one gulp.

Dullington would never let go of him. Never. His plans for Sparrow were too grand, too selfish to abandon. The vodka burned all the way down his throat, setting fire to his stomach. He grimaced, waiting for it to go to his head.

He spent the night on the floor, his feet facing the wall. He'd slept in the bed for two nights in a row. A third time might establish a routine, and he could not be too cautious. It was this caution which kept him out of the gray world, away from Dullington's reach. So far it worked, but he had to remain on his toes. He had to be ready. The whore was obvious, singling him out at the bar, her advances too strong. He'd had his share of whores, and Lanna wasn't one of them.

Nice try, Al. You'll have to try harder.

An image of Aleister Dullington sprang to mind. It prompted a chill that lingered in his old bones for hours. Dr. Albert Sparrow curled up in the coarse blankets, closed his eyes, and tried to sleep away waking memories of his years lost in the gray maze.

They were nightmares on tiny, white legs, and they followed him down into the depths of sleep.

-8-
CANDLES

THE STORM LET up as Donovan neared his brother's neighborhood. Remnants of thunder boomed in the distance, but the rain fell elsewhere, and he was grateful for its passing.

The flickering lingered after leaving the Monochrome. He hoped it would stop, as he'd found more excitement in the last several hours than he'd had in his whole life, but it did not relent. He felt its invisible hand pull at his stomach while the world around him slowly lost its color.

When it did, he saw dozens of Yawning standing along the sidewalks and streets. He passed through several of them, feeling a chill as he did.

Donovan tried to put the abominations out of his mind and focus on the task at hand instead. He wondered if Michael was even home. He'd tried calling again after returning to the car, but the call went straight to Michael's voicemail. Donovan knew his brother turned off his phone, especially on Friday evenings; however, he also knew Michael had to come home sometime, and decided he would wait his brother out.

When Donovan turned onto Michael's street, he was relieved to see he wouldn't be reduced to shivering on the curb. Lights glowed warmly from the windows of Michael's house, an expense Donovan knew his frugal brother wouldn't undertake unless he were home. Donovan parked along the curb and sat for a minute.

What if he doesn't believe me?

He looked down at the gun on the passenger seat. Could he put a gun to his own brother's head and force him to help? Joe Hopper's reassuring drawl piped up in his head: *Won't come to that, hoss.*

They spoke different languages, he and Michael, but Donovan had learned to adapt over the years. Michael Candle might not buy into the more sensational aspects of Donovan's story, but he would respond to Donna's abduction.

Donovan took the gun and got out of the car just as a strong gale swept down the center of the street. Thunder hammered farther out over the city. He shoved the gun in his jacket pocket and hurried up the sidewalk.

Donovan was calmed by the shifting, multi-colored glow of the television through the window. He hesitated for a moment, but remembered Dullington's words: *My cretins will not inhibit your progress.*

He pressed the doorbell, waiting a full minute for the door to finally swing open. Michael Candle stood before him in a green bathrobe sporting several days' growth of facial hair, clutching a bottle of beer in one hand.

"Don? What—"

But Donovan's mouth was dry, and words he'd imagined saying to his brother faltered on his tongue. His legs turned to jelly, and he all but collapsed at Michael's feet. The sobs came in long, whiny gusts. Michael stood over him, shocked, unsure of what to do or say. Finally he knelt and put a hand on Donovan's shoulder.

"Talk to me, man. I tried to call, but I couldn't get through on either line. What's going on?"

After a few seconds, Donovan collected himself, and looked up in his older brother's eyes. His jaw quivered.

"I need your help."

•

"Drink this." Michael handed him a tumbler of whiskey. "It'll warm you up."

Donovan sipped the drink, feeling its slow burn all the way down to his belly. Michael perched on the edge of his recliner, leaned forward, and picked up Guffin's weapon from the coffee table. He ejected the magazine and examined it.

He grunted. "No registration number. You realize how much trouble you'd be in if you were caught with this?"

"It doesn't matter," Donovan said. "No one can see me, anyway."

Michael returned the gun and stared at him. Donovan put down his drink.

"It's complicated."

"Try me."

"Fine."

Donovan told his story, starting with Monday's argument and finishing with his drive from the parking garage. Michael sat back, swallowed by the armchair's upholstery, and gave his brother a hard look.

"You . . . *do* understand how insane all of this sounds, right?"

Donovan nodded. He understood all too well. A shiver ripped its way through him, and he took another sip of the whiskey, relishing its fire on his tongue.

"I know how it sounds," he said, "but if you go to my house, you'll find that my wife is not there. The kitchen is a disaster. And Mr. Precious Paws—" He paused, recalling the cat's frightened, lifeless eyes. He took another drink. "My cat's dead."

"And you didn't call the cops?"

"No, I didn't call the cops. What the hell would I say to them? Honestly, Mike, if I called the damn cops, do you think they'd be hot on the case?" He waited. Michael didn't answer. "Exactly. I'd be sitting at the station, regurgitating my story over and over while they decide whether or not I'm out of my fucking mind."

"Don, *I* can't decide if you're crazy or not."

"Funny."

Michael smirked. "Y'know, I thought you were joking when I got your message earlier."

"Joking?" Donovan set down his glass with a loud clank. "Donna is fucking *gone*, Mike. My wife is—" He bit his lip. He couldn't bring himself to finish the sentence, and wasn't certain he wanted to.

Michael frowned. "I'm sorry, okay? I didn't mean it like that. All I meant was, nothing unexpected ever happens to you."

Donovan opened his mouth to speak, but stopped short. His brother was right, nothing unexpected ever happened to him. He'd lived his life in a safety net of his own construction, going about his days without so much as a variation in routine or structure. It had led him down this path, and now Donna's life was at stake because of it.

"Anyway, you've got a point about the cops. They'd have you locked up under suspicion while they search your house."

"That's why I called you instead. At least you'd hear me out before calling the men in white coats to carry me away."

Michael smirked. "Jury's still out on calling the men in white coats; your story's logic doesn't add up."

"My story's logic?"

"Yeah." Michael poured himself a glass of whiskey. "If you're flickering out, how come I can see and hear you? You said no one else could."

Always looking for the con. Donovan had to smile, but it quickly faded when he remembered Dullington's words. *My Cretins will not inhibit your progress.*

"I had reservations about coming here, about calling you, but Dullington knew that. The best I can figure is, you can see me because he wants you to see me." Donovan shrugged. "Otherwise, I haven't the slightest idea."

"Are you doing it now?"

"Doing what? Flickering?"

Michael nodded. He leaned forward, tumbler in hand, his eyes alight like a child waiting for a magic trick.

"Not right now. It's random. Sometimes it will be hours, and it will start up out of nowhere. Just like—"

Hiccups, he wanted to say, but the sensation silenced him in mid-sentence. His stomach knotted as color drained from the room.

Michael lost detail and form, reduced to a shadow, and no Cretin stood on his shoulder. This observation confirmed Donovan's suspicions: the Cretins made people oblivious.

When he flickered back, Donovan found his brother staring in shock. Michael's hands trembled.

"Mike?"

"You vanished. How did you do that?"

Donovan shrugged. "I told you, it's random. I can't shut it off."

Michael sat back in his chair. He drank his whiskey in a single gulp, grimacing as it burned its way down. He scrutinized Donovan, his eyes narrowing to an intense gaze. *He doesn't believe it*, Donovan realized. *Even after seeing it happen, he still doesn't believe it.* For a moment he was angry, but when he put himself in Michael's place, he realized he couldn't blame him.

"Mike, I know this might be difficult to believe—"

"Do you remember when we were in high school, and you had a hell of a time with calculus? You couldn't wrap your brain around it, no matter which way it was explained to you."

He did. Simple arithmetic was one thing, but math with numbers *and* letters still perplexed him.

"What's your point?"

"Whatever just happened to you," Michael went on, filling his glass, "well, I saw it. And I'll be damned if I understand it. Like it doesn't compute."

"Maybe you're not supposed to understand it."

"Maybe not, but it does tell me one thing about all of this." Michael took another drink. "It means you're not nearly as batshit crazy as I thought you were. Or if you are, it's contagious."

Donovan offered a faint smile. "Or genetic."

"That, too." Michael set down his glass. His hands were still shaking.

Donovan wanted to believe he was crazy, that this situation was a delusion concocted by his sick mind. That meant everything was fine, Donna was still home, safe and sound, their cat was still alive—

But that ain't the way it's goin', boss. You know it, 'n I know it.

Donovan did know it, and the knowledge left a bitter, metallic taste in his mouth. He reached for the bottle and poured himself another drink.

"So let's say you're not crazy, and I'm not crazy." Michael paused, smirking while Donovan tipped back the glass. He drained it in two swallows. "Go easy on that."

"I'm fine," Donovan said. He wiped his mouth. "You were saying?"

"Right. If we're not losing our minds, then it means what's happening is really happening. That means you're not bullshitting me."

Donovan nodded. "I wouldn't make this up."

"I know. That's what scares me." Michael paused, thinking. "This guy who took Donna, what did you say his name was?"

"George Guffin."

Michael rose from his armchair and left the room. He returned a minute later with a notepad and pen. He sat, scribbling across the top page.

"This Dullington guy—" Michael kept writing. "—did he give any indication as to who he's looking for?"

Donovan shook his head. "His protégé. No name. I think we'll find out tomorrow."

He watched Michael write, filling the page with a quick scrawl, pausing every few words to check the previous lines. His eyes darted up and down, double-checking himself. Donovan found it fascinating, watching his brother work, and he felt comforted by it. He recalled writing scenes with Joe Hopper, wondering how Michael might go about his work. He'd been too timid to ask, and he was happy to see that he got it right.

A few minutes and a full page later, Michael paused, looking up at his brother.

"Anything else?"

"No." Donovan gestured to the notepad. "What's all that?"

"My curiosity."

"What the hell does that mean?" Donovan watched Michael rise from his seat. He capped the bottle—now almost empty—and returned it to the kitchen.

"It means I've got work to do. Have you eaten anything?"

Donovan realized he hadn't since lunchtime, but all the panic had ruined any sort of appetite he might have had. The whiskey burned in his empty stomach. His head swam.

"No," he said, "but I'm not hungry."

"Well, there's food in the fridge if you *do* get hungry." Michael motioned to the stairs. "Come on."

"Where are we going?"

"*You're* going to bed. I'm going to check on some things."

"I can't—"

Michael smiled. "You need to sleep, Don. I don't know what you went through to get here, but you look like hell now. Go sleep. You need it."

Donovan fought back a yawn. He didn't like the prospect of sleep—not with Donna in captivity—but his brother had a point.

"Go to bed. I'll wake you first thing in the morning."

He followed Michael upstairs to the guest room. They stood in the doorway for a moment, unsure of what to say to one another. Donovan wanted to thank his brother, and the words were on his lips to do so, but Michael silenced him with a simple gesture. He put his hand on Donovan's shoulder.

"She's going to be okay, Don. We'll find her."

Donovan tried to smile. "I hope so, Mike."

He turned away before his brother could see the tears in his eyes. He closed the door, choking back the sadness and the sobs, and waited to hear his brother's descent before letting it out.

•

Michael went downstairs, checked the locks, and turned off the TV. He stood over the coffee table, staring at the tablet and his page of notes. George Guffin. The name had a familiar ring to it that wouldn't relent. It was somewhere in his head, buried deep enough that he couldn't quite retrieve it, but it nagged enough to let him know it was there.

The other name, however—Aleister Dullington—raised no flags. It was an odd name, almost too self-aware to believe given what his brother told him tonight. He still had a hard time buying it, but then he'd seen his brother disappear before his own eyes.

I'm just tired. Or maybe it's the liquor.

Maybe, but even that did not sit well with Michael Candle. He'd not hit the liquor until just before Donovan pulled his little vanishing act, and no amount of bourbon could affect him that quickly.

So what, then? Michael ran his hands through his hair, staring at his notes. He kept thinking about the way Donovan faded, the way he could see the sofa's texture through his brother's body. A chill crept its way up his spine.

Michael shook off the chills, took the tablet, and went into his home office. He flicked on a light, illuminating the tiny room. Each wall was lined with filing cabinets packed with stacks of files representing years of work. At the opposite end was his desk—heaped with files piled as tall as his computer monitor.

He'd long thought about expanding the business and renting office space, but had been too busy to follow through. Not that he minded. The money made being busy worth the lack of free time.

"Guffin," he said, turning to the cabinet drawer labeled "G." He opened it, rifling through the mess of folders until he came upon the name. "There you are."

The folder's contents were scant. It contained the requisite paperwork—filled out by Darlene Guffin, the man's sister—a few handwritten notes, a copy of the final invoice, and a single photograph clipped to the inside of the file. He moved into the light, stared at the man's pallid face, and thought about what Donovan told him. This Guffin fellow didn't even look capable of doing such things. He looked like a sneeze might knock him over.

Acts of coercion can change a man. He chewed his bottom lip and sat down at his desk, turning on his computer and waiting for it to boot.

Michael closed the folder and set it aside. *Donovan,* he thought, *what the hell have you gotten yourself into?*

He was used to his brother's fantastic stories. As children, Donovan used to tell Michael the wildest tales after bedtime. They were stories of superheroes, vigilantes, and inhuman creatures.

Monsters.

He frowned. Descriptions of this "Monochrome" reality

seemed like something his brother might concoct from his imagination. Donovan's insistence on wondering *What if?*, despite simpler, logical explanations, did not help matters. These Cretins, the Yawning, even Aleister Dullington—it was all too far-fetched, and yet—

He just vanished in front of me. In and out, completely transparent. Michael had read about tricks of light, even scientific experiments to bend it, but such things were the stuff of illusions and laboratories. Yet somehow, he had seen it happen less than four feet in front of him, in plain sight.

So what was it, then? Not a trick, certainly. And, he figured, it didn't matter. Regardless of this thing he'd witnessed—for which there *had* to be a logical explanation—the life of his sister-in-law was at stake. He'd never seen Donovan so troubled before in all their years. He was the most devoted person Michael knew, and his love for Donna was sacred. This was not something he would joke about. Its effect on him was apparent; Donovan looked like shit.

Michael leaned back in his chair, staring at the ceiling. He yawned. The liquor was getting to his brain, making things fuzzy around the edges. *Change tracks*, he thought, putting his hand on the mouse. He opened his web browser and searched for "Aleister Dullington."

Zero hits. He looked down at his notes, then tried another entry: "Monochrome."

There were too many entries to sort through.

What did Donovan call it? Right, the "flickering."

Michael searched for the term. Again, it yielded too many results. It was already late, and the whiskey was pulling at his eyes. He tried one more phrase: "Monochrome + Flickering."

Another grouping of results popped up, but halfway down the page, one caught his eye. It was from a book excerpt: "It is the point at which a man throws off his shackles and declares 'No more.' He must justify himself in the face of flickering anonymity, lest he be subjugated to an eternity of monochrome oblivion."

Michael's curiosity was piqued. He clicked the link, which directed him to an online retailer offering a discount on the book *A Life Ordinary: A Comprehensive Study in Human Mediocrity*. The same quote was farther down the page, along with a photo of its author. He was a smug-looking fellow with salt-and-pepper hair tied back into a ponytail. His eyes were a cool blue, and he wore a smirk that left Michael frowning.

He scribbled some more notes on his tablet. "Now we're getting somewhere."

•

Sleep came instantly, but Donovan was haunted by a myriad of dreams that dug up the day's remains. He saw Aleister Dullington's grinning face, its lidless eyes peering out at him from a shroud of blackness. At first, his dream-self thought the face was just an image, a tapestry hung upon some vast wall. Then the eyes moved and the mouth opened, bellowing laughter both mechanical and human. It was the sound of the Cretins, their voices like records played backwards, coupled with the grinding, screeching sound of rusted metal against metal. A low, electronic drone filled the spaces in between, twisting together, culminating into an ominous wave. It thickened the air, and Donovan felt himself swallowing quicksand he could not see.

Dullington opened his mouth, spilling out a seemingly endless sea of Cretins and Yawning like gobs of mucus. Donovan stood, rooted in place by an invisible hand which squeezed him, expelling the air from his lungs. He found he could not blink, and his heart pounded with fury, threatening to burst from his chest.

Looking down, Donovan saw his skin bulge. There was no pain. He watched in silence as his chest cracked, splintering into thin red lines that crawled outward. Each breath spread them wider, allowing his heart to beat its way out of captivity. It flopped down onto the black floor below.

The open wound sealed, yet Donovan's heart continued its rhythm, beating a counterpoint to the terror coursing through his mind. He tried to speak, but found he could not. Dullington leered at him, a disembodied face against the darkened shroud. Donovan wanted to look away, but no matter where he looked Dullington was there, grinning.

Who are you, Mr. Candle? I will tell you. A nothing-man, with a nothing-face and a nothing-life. A liar unto yourself; you are a great deceiver.

No, Donovan thought, *I'm not a liar.*

Dullington's face bulged and broke, splitting at seams around his eyes, down the sides of his nose, and into his mouth. A pale, gray sludge gushed out of the seams as his skin peeled back, revealing meat and muscle underneath.

You are, Mr. Candle. There are no greater lies than those you tell yourself.

His black eyes fell from their sockets and rolled over a throng of Cretins. Donovan watched as one of the eyeballs moved past and into the darkness. *I see you,* it whispered, *and you see me, see you, see me, see you . . .*

Donovan felt a sharp tug at his face, followed by a low, wet, tearing sound. A piece of his skin fell from his cheek, landing with a sickening plop.

Donovan wanted to scream, but his mouth would not move. His lips detached from his skull to join the pile of flesh at his feet.

I will show you, Mr. Candle. You will see there is nothing underneath you but a waste of flesh and a wealth of lies.

I'm not a liar, Donovan wanted to cry, but his body's actions were no longer his own. He stepped outside of himself, becoming an observer as his body tore itself apart one piece at a time. The visage was one of meat and bone, devoid of flesh, eyes inset in a state of constant shock.

From these ghoulish remains came a voice. "I am perfectly content."

There came an airy pop as each of his eyes plopped from his head and dangled just below his nose.

Don, he heard a voice say.

Donovan.

He tried to scream as his former self decayed before him, but he found himself unable to make utterance. There existed only the hushed sound of movement, of little legs scampering across the black divide.

"Donovan, wake up."

The Cretins swarmed the pile of flesh at his feet, consuming his remains. The last thing he heard before consciousness pulled him from that black abyss was the sound of Dullington laughing—not from somewhere else, somewhere above or around—but from within.

•

Donovan squinted, rubbed his eyes, and looked up. Michael stared down at him, a mug in his hand.

"You okay?"

Pale light filtered through the window. He looked around the room, confused about how he got there. Fragments of the dream clung to his conscious mind, taunting him with flashes of Aleister Dullington and his monochromatic minions. Donovan ran a hand across his face, feeling for scars left by his nightmare, but it just came away wet with perspiration.

"Don?"

The previous day rushed back to him. He frowned, shook off the dream, and let out slow yawn.

"You were struggling in your sleep. I heard you talking."

Donovan thought of the nightmare, fighting back a chill.

"I'm okay," he said. "What time is it?"

Michael placed the mug on the nightstand and sat on the edge of the bed.

"It's almost ten."

"Did anyone—"

"No one's called." Michael pointed to the mug. "I made you some coffee. I hope you like it black."

Donovan sat up, leaned against the headboard, and reached for the mug. It was bitter and burned his tongue, but he didn't mind. Michael yawned, and Donovan noticed the scruff on his face.

"You look like shit."

Michael smirked. "Thanks. I'm usually not up this early on a Saturday."

"Still a night owl?"

"Always." Michael got up, went to the door. "I did a little digging last night, found some things. It's downstairs, for when you're ready."

Donovan took another sip of the coffee. He climbed out of

bed and stood at the window, gazing out at the overcast morning. The surrounding neighborhood was affluent, with SUVs and sports cars in the driveways of cookie-cutter homes as far as he could see. He remembered his dream—*I am perfectly content*—and frowned, thinking about how he used to pine to live in such a place.

But that's not you, boss. Never was.

It wasn't. He wasn't sure who he was anymore, but he knew who he'd become was not the man he wanted to be.

A bird cawed overhead. Across the street, one of Michael's neighbors got in a car and backed out of their driveway. Life went about its business, oblivious to the gray layers underneath.

He thought of Donna, cursing himself for bringing all this upon her.

"I'm sorry," he whispered. Tears welled up in his eyes, but he wouldn't let them come. He'd done his share of crying. No more.

He stepped into the bathroom to refresh, then went downstairs to look for his brother. The light was on in Michael's office, and he entered to find him sitting at the computer, surrounded by filing cabinets and stacks of files. Donovan surveyed the room, recalling how messy his brother had been, and smiling at how things never seemed to change. There were stalagmites of paper rising from the floor of the office cave, mute testaments to Michael's years spent as a private investigator.

"You've been busy."

Michael looked up, surprised, then noticed Donovan's gaze directed at the surrounding disorganization. He shrugged. "It's a living."

"What did you find?" He peered over Michael's shoulder at the open file in his hand. There was a photo clipped to the inside, and he recognized Guffin's face immediately. He doubted he would ever forget. "You had a file on him?"

Michael handed him the folder. "Missing Persons case from a few years ago." He motioned to the stacks. "Most of these are Missing Persons cases. Been my bread 'n butter for a long time."

Donovan forgot about Guffin's file for a moment, looking at the folders stacked upon one another. Something stuck in his brain, tickling the same place where he'd constructed Joe Hopper.

"All of these people are missing?"

Michael nodded. "I usually get five or six calls a day. A kid who's run away, or a spouse who's fled town. Sometimes it's an estranged family member who fell out of the picture."

"Do you ever find them?"

"Sometimes," Michael said, separating a stack of papers into smaller, manageable portions. "Other times, it's like they just vanished—"

They shared an unsettling glance for a moment before Donovan cleared his throat and looked down at Guffin's photo. It was a professional portrait, revealing a well-groomed man with thick glasses. He wore a gray suit and red tie. It was the kind of photo that might hang in a corporate lobby, and Donovan had seen his share hanging in the entrance to the Identinel offices. Staring at the photo reminded Donovan that Guffin was once a normal man—not a wife-abducting cat-killer.

In this snapshot, Guffin feigned pride and happiness with a thin, false smile. It was a smile Donovan knew. He'd worn it himself on many occasions, and it made him sick to think of it.

He opened the folder and read over the report. Guffin was last seen four years ago on his way to work for Brooks & Foster, a local accounting firm. Unmarried, no friends, with no discernable hobbies—George Guffin was an empty silhouette of a man.

Donovan looked at his brother. "Do you remember anything about this?"

"Vaguely. There wasn't much to work with. He left for work one day and never got there. Never returned home. *Poof.* Gone."

Donovan remembered the desperate look in Guffin's eye, the way he screamed in fear as the world changed around them. *There are others like you 'n me. He lets us out sometimes, only lets people see us when he wants them to.*

He went to the nearest stack and opened one folder after another. Each contained the same forms—invoices, expense sheets, photographs, testimonials—filed by family or friends desperate to find their missing loved ones. He looked at each photo. Most were adults, men and women from all corners of life, possessed of a smile that betrayed them. *They aren't happy*, he thought. *Not really.*

And now he's got 'em, boss.

Donovan flickered without realizing it. The stack of papers dimmed, and when color returned to the room, he found Michael staring at him.

"I see it happen," he said, "but it still doesn't compute."

"Sorry." Donovan returned the stack of folders. "It's not easy for me, either." He noticed a few sheets of paper in Michael's hand. "What's that?"

"Something else I think you need to see. Decided to search a bit online, and—"

The phone startled them. Their eyes met.

"Hang on." Michael turned in his chair, found the cell phone under a pile of junk mail, and silenced it. He turned back to his brother. "Anyway—"

Donovan's pocket vibrated, catching him off guard. He'd forgotten about his own phone. However, when he retrieved it, he found the screen was blank. The battery had been almost dead the day before, and leaving it on overnight had surely drained it. Still, the phone vibrated, sounding its polyphonic tones in rising scale.

Michael's cell phone rang again, joining the chorus. For a moment, Donovan was overcome with panic. Should he answer? Should Michael answer? The ringing continued, and finally the brothers answered their phones in tandem.

Static greeted Donovan's ear. He could hear the same echoing from his brother's phone. Michael heard it, too, and mouthed *What the hell?* Donovan shrugged.

A familiar voice formed out of the static, and Donovan felt a lump rise in his throat.

"Brothers Candle," said Aleister Dullington. "Good morning to you both."

•

His voice came out of both phones, creating a reverb effect that mimicked the odd language of the Cretins. Michael shot a glance at his brother.

"Mr. Dullington."

"Did you sleep well, Mr. Candle?"

"Well enough."

"I am disappointed, Mr. Candle. You have not yet introduced me to your brother. But that is no matter, I am well aware of him."

The brothers looked at one another. This time it was Michael who shrugged.

"Yes, Michael Candle, I know all about you." Static crackled through the line, accenting Dullington's voice, lowering it into a growl. "You and I are natural enemies."

Michael cleared his throat. "Is that so?"

"Quite. You seek those who are missed, while I facilitate the missing." Dullington chuckled. "In some ways, we perpetuate a cycle. You may consider it *good business*."

Donovan cut in. "Get to the point, Mr. Dullington. Who do you need me to find?"

"And why don't you do it yourself, Al?" Michael snapped. Donovan shook his head. *Shut up, Mike, keep your damn mouth shut for once.* He thought about knocking the phone from Michael's hand. His brother's smartass tone had landed him in plenty of trouble over the years, mostly with their parents, but this time it was for keeps.

"Shall I make your brother a bargaining chip in this affair?" Dullington's voice was solemn, resigned. "It can be arranged."

"No," Donovan said, staring hard at his brother. "That won't be necessary."

"Good. I seek a man named Albert Sparrow. You are to find him and bring him to me."

Michael looked down at the pages in his hand. Donovan saw they were trembling. The name rang a bell, but he couldn't place it. It was there in the back of his brain, swimming around, avoiding his grasp.

"Who is he?"

"That is no concern of yours, Mr. Candle. You are to simply find him and deliver him unto me."

"But where—"

"There is a reason I freed your brother from the grip of the Cretins, Mr. Candle. He is a detective, is he not? A good one, by my understanding. After all, isn't that why you modeled your own character after him?"

Donovan's face flushed with embarrassment. The secret of Joe Hopper was something he'd never told his brother, but now that game was up. He felt exposed. Michael shot him a wry smirk before returning his attention to the phone.

"Where do we take this guy once we find him?" Michael asked. "And what if he doesn't want to join us?"

Static hissed through the line once more, distorting Dullington's voice.

"I *guarantee* he will not go with you willingly. He knows what awaits him on the other side. It is why he ran, and that is your problem to solve. Mr. Candle—"

Donovan closed his eyes. "Yes?"

"Have you given any more thought to my question?"

For a moment Donovan wasn't sure what he was talking about, but then he remembered the dream, and the long day preceding it. He hesitated, not sure how to respond.

"It is no matter, Mr. Candle. You still have time to answer— and you *will* have to answer. For now I leave you brothers to your task. Good day."

The resounding surge of digital noise made both men pull away from their phones. Michael sat back in his chair and stared down at the floor.

"What did he mean? What question?"

Donovan leaned against one of the cabinets and shook his head. "It's nothing." He pointed to the pages in Michael's hand. "You were going to show me something else?"

"I was, but your friend beat me to it." Michael handed him the papers. They were print-outs about Dr. Sparrow's book, his photograph, and a list of tour dates. "Seems we have a common interest."

He scanned the itinerary, pausing at the current date: Sparrow was in town. Donovan looked up at his brother. Michael grinned.

"Want to go meet a celebrity?"

•

Michael took a bite of his breakfast sandwich. They had an hour to kill before Sparrow's event, and their growling stomachs mandated a stop for food. They sat in the car on the second level of a parking garage a block from the bookstore.

"So what's this about 'modeling your character' after me?"

The question took Donovan by surprise, and for a moment he didn't understand its context. His mind was elsewhere, away from the demands of his ravenous body and the imminent confrontation with Dr. Sparrow. He was focused on his wife, all the things he feared he'd never get to say to her.

"Modeling my character?" He thought for a moment. "Oh. *That.*"

A cloud of heat covered his face. *Oh boy,* he thought. He'd expected the conversation, but not so soon. He pictured Dullington somewhere in the Monochrome, grinning.

"Well?" Michael jabbed Donovan's arm. "Come on, out with it."

"All right. This book I'm working on is about a detective."

A thin smile spread across Michael's face. "Go on."

Donovan imagined Joe Hopper, his face cast in a permanent five o'clock shadow, cigarette hanging limp from the corner of his mouth. He thought about Hopper's early life, the life written nowhere else but in Donovan's own mind. *Might as well go 'n tell 'em, boss.*

"His name is Joe Hopper. He's a gruff son of a bitch. Southern stock. Tough guy. He's searching for someone."

"Who?"

Donovan smiled, feeling excited about his story for the first time in days. "For a woman. A lady by the name of Mistress Colby."

"Her first name is Mistress?"

"Sort of. Haven't worked that bit out just yet."

"When were you going to tell me about this?"

He sighed. "I don't know, Mike. The novel's been in and out of the works for years now. I guess I didn't want you to know until it was done."

Michael finished his sandwich and wiped his chin. "Are you going to try and get it published? That's still your dream, isn't it?"

Here we go, Donovan thought. *It always comes back to this.*

"Yeah," he said. "Some day."

"How long have you been working on it?"

Donovan thought for a moment. "About seven years, I think."

"So why not finish it?"

"Real-life matters. Work, sleep, that sort of thing. Necessary distractions, I guess. And—" He stopped to think for a moment. What was it that he'd found so wrong with the novel almost a week ago? It was too predictable, too bland. He realized that it was nothing more than a reflection of his own life. Joe Hopper was based on his brother, but on another level, he was based on Donovan's own yearning for the things he lacked: something different, something adventurous, something more fulfilling than the nine-to-five grind he had lived every single day for the last nine years. In the face of his desire he'd deleted the document, frustrated with its lack of direction.

Only now did he realize that frustration stemmed from something far more prevalent than a collection of words. It sickened him when he realized this terrible incident had been necessary to understanding his own pathology.

"And?"

Donovan looked up from his breakfast. He'd lost his appetite. "And the story was just empty, anyway. Dull. Kind of like me."

"You really think so?"

He nodded. "I do. Took me too long to figure that out."

"Well, aren't you supposed to write what you know? Don't take this the wrong way, but you're not exactly the most exciting person in the world, Don."

Michael's words stung, but Donovan did not try to defend himself. He knew his brother was right. It was a harsh truth he had to face, and it wasn't easy. He returned to a fact that haunted him: his delusion of happiness and contentment was the cause of Donna's abduction. His stomach tied itself into a series of knots.

"You always nagged me for not taking more chances. I always wanted to play it safe, and now it's come back to bite me on the ass.

This is all my fault."

Michael was quiet. He balled up the greasy wrapper and tossed it into the fast food bag.

"I nagged you because I wanted to see you do better. Our folks were always at work, slaving away at their jobs to make it better for us, and I didn't want us to resign ourselves to that kind of life. I expected more from you because I *knew* you could do more."

Donovan turned away, staring out the window at empty rows and concrete columns.

"I won't bullshit you, Don. If what you told me is real, then yeah, this is nothing else but your own fault for being a boring guy. But—" Michael drummed his fingers along the steering wheel. "—self-pity isn't going to help you. It's going to drive you deeper into the hole you're already in. You need to focus. For Donna, and for yourself. Got it?" He reached out and put his hand on Donovan's shoulder. "And for what it's worth, I really dig your story idea. I'd like to read it someday."

"Thanks, Mike. For everything."

"Don't mention it."

The brothers shared a smile. It lasted only a moment, but it was long enough. Afterward, Michael started the car and turned on the heater. There was still time before the book signing, and he saw no sense in freezing. Donovan reached over and turned on the radio. A blast of rock music startled him, the industrial noise of Nine Inch Nails making his head hurt. He cringed at the synthetic drones. It reminded him too much of the Monochrome, and he quickly changed the station.

"—ame is Alice Walenta. She is 5'9", roughly 150 lbs, and has long, black hair. If you or anyone you know has information of her whereabouts—"

Her grainy photo from the newspaper sprang to mind. He used to ignore the Missing Persons reports, but in light of his new suspicions, it chilled him to think about how many reports he'd seen and heard over the years. *How many people disappear every day?* he wondered. *How many end up with Dullington?*

His gut clenched, accenting his thought with a brief shift of the world's color. The interior of Michael's car vanished for a moment, leaving Donovan hovering between Spectrum and Monochrome. There were Cretins standing watch along the garage floor.

When he flickered back, he found Michael changing the station. He hadn't noticed Donovan's brief disappearance. Donovan leaned his head against the window and stared out, his thoughts drifting back to the task at hand.

Fear inched its way up within him, coiling around his stomach. What if Dullington was lying and all this was just a game? He remembered the way Dullington frowned when he asked about Sparrow: anger was one of the few emotions he'd witnessed splashed across the pale canvas of Dullington's face.

No, he thought. *Dullington's not lying. He's too particular, a devil for the details. Manipulative, yes, but not a liar.*

His thoughts turned to Sparrow. He wondered what a man could possibly do to inspire such resentment and determination from a being like Aleister Dullington? Furthermore, what kind of man was capable of such a thing?

Donovan looked at the dashboard clock. He would find out in fewer than twenty minutes.

-9-
THE GOOD DOCTOR

THE DOOR WAS open when Donna woke. She tried to roll on her side and pull up her knees to conserve body heat. It was freezing, and when she opened her eyes, the faint orange glow from the fire was no longer present. She couldn't hear its distant crackle and pop, either.

She could hear something else: voices coming from outside. They spoke in hushed tones, and she strained to listen. It sounded like men talking, but she didn't recognize any of them.

"—supposed to happen today."

"You sure?"

"Yeah, that's the word. Old Dull's got a lot of faith in this Candle guy."

"What's so special about Sparrow, anyway?"

"The ones who've been here the longest—"

"The ones who haven't wasted away to nothing, you mean."

"—right, them. They say Sparrow used to be one of us, but he found a way to escape. Dullington had plans for him, something different than the rest of us, and he's been after him ever since."

"How long?"

"Who knows. Years, probably."

"Jesus."

The names, however, she recognized. She'd heard Dullington and Sparrow whispered about in the dark, through the closed door, and she wondered how her husband was mixed up in their affairs. He lived a quiet life and never bothered anyone. How had he crossed paths with these people?

Donna closed her eyes and thought of Donovan. She feared for him, feared what might happen if he couldn't do whatever was expected of him.

He'll find his way, she reminded herself, *he always does*. It was meager comfort, but she clung to it, ignoring the pangs of hunger in her belly and the sting of her bladder.

The thought kept her warm in the bitter dark. She cherished it. It was all she had left.

•

The brothers waited for the crosswalk light to change. Across the street, a line of patrons stretched beyond the doors of Harrison & Main Booksellers and wound its way around the corner. Michael nudged Donovan and pointed toward the crowd.

"Do you think your book could sell this much?"

Donovan shot his brother a quick smirk. "No way. This self-help crap always sells more."

"Sounds like you're in the wrong business."

"Maybe I am." He observed another large group join the line from an adjacent street as traffic inched through the intersections. A breeze picked up around them, and the city's colors shifted, losing depth and focus, allowing Donovan to see a different sort of crowd gathering outside the building. A few Yawning loitered in the middle of the street, towering over a churning sea of Cretins.

Looks like the whole fan club's here.

They vanished and were replaced by two lanes of traffic. The traffic signal indicated it was safe to cross. Donovan took a breath, fixed his eyes on the bookstore, and made his way to the other side. Michael followed.

"Have you thought about what you're going to say to this guy?"

Donovan stopped at the opposite sidewalk and looked at the line. It ran the full length of the building. Michael grabbed his arm.

"Don? Did you hear me?"

"I did," he said, "and I don't know. It's not every day I have to tell a man I've been sent to kidnap him, y'know?"

"Well, you'd better think on your feet. This thing's supposed to start soon, and the line's not getting any shorter."

Michael was right. Donovan couldn't see the end of the line, and he knew the bookstore was not very large. He looked to the entrance and smiled.

"I think I have an idea."

He walked away from his brother, toward the front of the line. Michael called out to him.

"Well? Are you going to share?"

Donovan looked back. "Go get in line, Mike. I'll see you inside."

A force swelled within him as the invisible hand clutched at his stomach, pulling him out of the Spectrum. Michael watched his brother vanish, and shook his head.

"I hope you know what you're doing," he muttered, shoving his hands in his pockets. He went to the back of the line.

•

In the span of minutes since his last view of the Monochrome, Donovan saw there were even more of the pale horrors. The street appeared to squirm as though covered in a thick layer of white insects. The mass was punctuated by even more Yawning, staggering over their tiny counterparts. In that moment, caught between both realities, Donovan heard their chattering cacophony with frightening clarity.

They're waiting.

Ahead, two Yawning stood guard at the entrance. Donovan held his breath as he passed between them. The last time he was this close to one it had been trying to eat him, so he made a point of hurrying through the entryway. He positioned himself between the outlines of two figures, each with a Cretin on their shoulder. They looked up at him and grinned.

Donovan winced. The foyer sprang to life as he flickered back. He stood between two women, neither of which paid him any notice. They each held a copy of Sparrow's book. Donovan scrutinized a promotional poster on the wall.

A Life Ordinary: A Comprehensive Study in Human Mediocrity. The title bled pretension, printed in bold letters across a sketched outline of a light bulb, with Sparrow's name aligned at the top. A blurb read, "A revolution in human progression." Donovan doubted that was actually the case, but the turnout for the day's event proved he was one of a small minority.

The line did not move for twenty minutes. Outside, police waved people through the intersections, the streets now at a standstill. Watching the urban chaos, Donovan thought, *I want this guy's publicist.*

He wondered what he would say to Dr. Sparrow. What *could* he say? *Hi, I'm Donovan Candle, and Aleister Dullington sent me to find you because, if I don't, he's going to kill my wife.* It was to the point, but sounded ridiculous in his head. He didn't know if Sparrow would even see him.

Doubt you'd be invisible to him, boss. He's public enemy numero uno in Monochrome land.

His mind raced with possibilities—what might happen if Sparrow didn't cooperate—but a push from behind displaced such thoughts. The line was moving. A woman bumped into him, confused, and her eyes glazed over when he tried to apologize. She squinted, straining to see him. Donovan shut his mouth and started walking.

He moved through the foyer, past a counter of cash registers, and worked his way through the crowd. Rows of bookshelves had been rearranged for the event, and in the center of the clearing was a lectern. A small group of chairs were claimed by those at the front of the line, leaving the rest to stand and fill out the store to its capacity. Donovan found a spot close to the lectern, just behind the last row of seats.

Then he saw the doctor, and his heart inched its way into his throat. His blood pressure spiked.

Dr. Albert Sparrow was a tall man. He wore a three-piece suit, colored gray to match silver hair pulled back into a ponytail. A thick mustache adorned his upper lip, accenting a grin which now spread across his face.

Sparrow swaggered to the lectern, taking the microphone in hand with the confidence of a rock star. The audience erupted with applause. Sparrow basked in it, listening to the cheers.

He leaned into the microphone and said, "I'm sorry, I didn't catch that. Come again?" The crowd ate it up, cheering and whistling. Donovan inferred two things from the man at that point: he adored the attention, and he knew how to manipulate. Dullington's interest in him was obvious.

Sparrow reached into his suit coat and pulled out a pair of glasses. As he did, a woman in a black dress walked to the lectern and whispered in his ear. He nodded, leaned in to the microphone and cleared his throat.

"Excuse me. I need your attention for a moment." Sparrow's voice boomed over the sound system. Most of the crowd's cheers slowly died down. "I'm sorry to be the bearer of bad news, but it appears the store is at capacity. I'm afraid if we let anyone else in here, we'll be in violation of the fire code."

Donovan turned and saw the entrance doors were closed, an angry mob of readers peering inside. A scan of those who got through revealed Michael was not among them.

Looks like I'm on my own, he thought.

"I'd like to welcome you, and to thank you for coming out and joining me today. As most of you probably know, my name is Dr. Albert Sparrow."

More cheers came from the audience. Donovan remained unimpressed. He hoped that if he ever made it as an author, he wouldn't be as pompous as this man. Sparrow's smile was that of a man full of himself; worse, it was the smile of a man at the height of power, one who knew he could say whatever he wanted and these people would still cheer for him.

"First, I will read from our favorite book for thirty minutes, after which I'll take a few questions. Then we'll move on to the signing. And if you didn't bring your copy, don't worry—the store has plenty in stock."

Sparrow held up a hardcover copy of the book. He adjusted his glasses, cleared his throat once more, and opened to a bookmarked page.

The gray sight overcame Donovan, and he witnessed something that left him dumbstruck. While the rest of the store shifted into varying shades of gray, the good doctor remained in full clarity, standing like a Technicolor beacon in a silent film. All around him, Cretins cringed as he spoke. His voice was garbled in the droning language of the Monochrome.

Hints of the Spectrum bled through the gray haze, and Sparrow's voice became clear as Donovan's gray sight relented.

"'—apter one: The Disease. There are two sides to every coin: light and dark, day and night, good and evil if one is inclined to take it that far. As human beings, we restrict ourselves to one side at a time. We wake up in the morning, we have breakfast, we kiss our spouses goodbye and we travel off to work. Then, at the end of the day, we come home, we have dinner, we relax, we sleep. Over the course of time, however, the human mind begins to fit this self-imposed mold—an act which it is not meant to perform, as this routine causes a state of banal atrophy.

"'Unfortunately this is a common side-effect of the nine-to-five grind. The human existence isn't meant to be confined to a box, a computer screen, a telephone, or any other device for a large amount of time. We begin to lose touch with reality, with our loved-ones, with our own lives. Mediocrity is a disease of our society, and unlike diseases of the natural world, this one is entirely man-made. Affliction is a choice.

"'Over the course of this study, three distinct 'life' dichotomies will be discussed in further detail, but for the purposes of this introduction, each will be broached so as to set the proverbial stage.'"

Sparrow paused, turning the page. Someone behind Donovan coughed. The rest of the audience was silent, hanging on the doctor's every word.

"'A life ordinary is the setting in which most of us live our lives. It is not aware of the layers underneath or above; rather, it is merely aware of itself and its own formulaic devices. A life ordinary plots itself from point A to B to C and beyond, until it reaches a point at which the obvious choice is to return to A, and so the poisonous cycle repeats until death. Over the course of this life, offspring are taught to live the same lifestyle, propagating yet another ordinary, banal existence.

"'However, there are grave consequences for some of those who choose to follow this bleak path to its destination.'"

Donovan listened, understanding creeping into his mind. He could see the road Sparrow was traveling, and it looked very familiar.

"'Some of us bury ourselves in our jobs, becoming machines of a sort, built with only one purpose—to do more work. Others may devote their lives to one thing, shutting out all of life's delights and interesting quirks. Some choose to convolute the very essence of humanity by saturating themselves with mediocrity. At this point, a life ordinary deteriorates into a life transparent.

"'A life transparent is a life in flux and transition. It is a liminal state, fraught with confusion and despair, attributed to a constant feeling of ennui. Most times, however, when one enters this stage it is too late for recourse. A person living a life transparent stands upon the threshold of decision: to vanish into obscurity, continuing on their self-destructive journey into a monochromatic version of the world devoid of life and warmth, ignored by those around them; alternatively, a person living a life transparent may take a road less traveled, if they recognize the symptoms early on.

"'A drastic change in lifestyle is necessary. This requires identifying the source of mediocrity and expelling it from daily life. It could mean changing one's job, finding a new hobby, or eliminating any other malignant preoccupation. Only then can one find the means with which to breach the veil and reenter the world's spectrum. It is through this 'life pitch,' so to speak, that one may leap from the precipice of virtual anonymity, transcending through a subset of dichotomies—hesitation, penitence, liminality, definition—and land safely in the shoes of a life random.'"

Dr. Sparrow looked up for a moment, adjusting his glasses, and he locked eyes with Donovan. Sparrow's face reddened. Donovan might as well have been the only person in the room. He felt exposed. The doctor's sharp glare left little room for denial: he could see Donovan just fine.

•

The man in the crowd caught Sparrow off guard, threw him off his game. He always prepared for the worst, expecting that Dullington might send an army to any one of the stops on his publicity tour, but until that moment he'd not yet encountered them. There were others, of course, but they always came before or after his public appearances, turning up in airport bars or at restaurants, trying to pass themselves off as fans.

Sparrow could easily spot them. There was always the tell-tale signs of dirt under the nails, hair that hadn't been washed in weeks or months, a foul stench. Lately, Dullington had taken to giving them the means to disguise themselves—even the whore had dressed her part—but this man in the crowd was different.

He didn't look like one of Dullington's puppets. At a glance, he looked like a normal fellow, but the longer Sparrow stared, the more he recognized the quiet desperation in the man's eyes. More importantly, the man noticed Sparrow could see him.

For a moment, Sparrow faltered at the lectern. A cold sweat broke out on his forehead, and the gun holstered inside his coat pulled at him. Paranoia swept over him in a heated wave.

He felt the room shift around him, felt the wrenching pull in his torso. It was a cold reminder of what awaited him if he let it catch up. *I won't go back*, he thought. *Never.* He locked eyes once more with the man in the audience, trying his best to transmit a warning across the space between them.

Do not fuck with me.

Sparrow returned to the book, and read to the end of the chapter.

•

The audience applauded as Dr. Sparrow finished the reading. Donovan had observed a change in the doctor's demeanor since they locked eyes: he was less boisterous than when he'd first approached the lectern, and when the crowd saw fit to give him a standing ovation, he had merely thanked them.

A moment later he excused himself, motioning to the woman in the black dress. She took his place at the microphone.

"It will be just a few minutes before we conclude with the Q&A."

Donovan kept his eye on Sparrow. The old man walked along the back wall toward a short hallway. A sign hung above the opening that read "Restrooms."

Better now than never, he thought. Donovan pushed his way through the crowd, circumventing the lectern and following after his target. He jogged through a maze of bookshelves, past a group of store clerks, and into the hall. Entrances to both restrooms stood opposite one another. A third door, labeled "Employees Only," stood at the end of the hall.

The door to the men's room swung to a close. Donovan pushed it open and stepped inside. Dr. Albert Sparrow ran water in the sink. He let it pool in his hands before wiping down his face and forehead. He looked sallow under the fluorescent lights. They aged him twenty years.

He dabbed his face with a handkerchief, pausing long enough to regard Donovan in the mirror.

"Can I help you?"

Donovan blinked, searching for the right words.

"Aleister Dullington sent me."

"Of course he did." Sparrow looked down at the sink, then into the mirror. He smiled, shaking his head. "This will never end, will it?"

Donovan wasn't sure what to say. He shifted his weight from one foot to the other, uncomfortable with the situation. Dr. Sparrow now appeared old, feeble, far from the smug bastard he'd made himself out to be.

"I'm so tired of this." He looked up at Donovan and put on his glasses. "Would you mind accompanying an old man to his car? I need my medication. This old heart isn't what it used to be."

Donovan agreed, following the doctor out into the hallway. They turned left through the Employees Only area, passing a small lounge and entering a loading zone filled with boxes of books. Donovan paid little attention to anything but the old man, the way his silver ponytail swished back and forth as he walked. He feared that if he took his eyes off the man, Sparrow would disappear.

They exited the building at the far side, stepping out into a wide alley. There was a silver BMW parked alongside the loading dock, marked with out-of-state plates and flagged with a rental company's logo. Donovan wasn't surprised by the car's elegance; it was just what he imagined a man like Sparrow might drive.

"Dr. Sparrow," Donovan began, "listen. I need to—"

"Please, son. Spare me. I'm sure whatever story he's given you to justify your actions helps you sleep at night, but it won't work with me. Just let me have my medicine before you do what it is you've come to do."

"You know why I'm here?"

Dr. Sparrow reached into his pocket and pulled out a set of keys. He disengaged the lock, prompting the car to chirp in agreement, and walked around to the passenger side door. Donovan stopped at the trunk. He wanted to plead with the man, explain the situation. Together, maybe they could find some sort of solution. Something that would work in their favor.

"Been after me for years," Sparrow mumbled. The old man turned, looking first to the alley's entrance, then back at its exit. "I've learned a thing or two along the way."

Donovan said nothing. He approached the side of the car. "Look, Dr. Sparrow, this is about my w—"

Donovan Candle suddenly found himself staring down the barrel of a gun.

-10-
NEGATIVE SPACES

At first Donovan wasn't sure what to do or say. Even after facing George Guffin and narrowly escaping the Yawning, he still found it difficult to suppress his bladder at the sight of a gun pointed at his face.

"I've learned not to trust a single fucking thing any of you rubes say. I don't care why you're here, or what he's promised you in return—I'm not going back, and I'll do whatever I have to do to keep it that way." Sparrow pressed the barrel harder against Donovan's skull. "Do you understand *that*, son?" His elderly demeanor was gone, and Donovan realized it had all been a ruse. "I'm going to remove you from this equation just like the rest of them, and—"

"Put it down, old man."

Sparrow's eyes widened at the sound of a cocked hammer. Michael Candle pressed the revolver into the back of Sparrow's silver mane.

Donovan's legs nearly gave out as the adrenaline slowed. "Mike, thank God."

"I said put it down."

Sparrow looked ahead, his eyes possessed with hatred more vicious than Donovan had ever seen. It made his cheeks burn. He almost wanted to apologize to the man, but the look in Sparrow's eyes made him hold his tongue.

The old man licked his lips and spoke evenly through clenched teeth. "Well played." He lowered the gun. Michael reached over, took it from Sparrow, and shoved it into his jacket pocket.

"Got anything else up your sleeve, old man?"

"No," Sparrow said, "I don't."

"Then you won't mind if I pat you down." Michael was quick about it. He came up empty handed. "Get in the car."

Sparrow's eyes darkened. He did not look back at Michael, but forward, glaring into Donovan's eyes. "I didn't catch your name, son."

"My name is Donovan Candle."

A thin smile cut across Sparrow's face. "Mr. Candle," he said, "I'm going to remember you."

Likewise, Donovan thought. Michael opened the door and shoved the doctor inside. He looked up at his brother.

"You okay?"

"Yeah," Donovan said. He looked at Michael's revolver. "Do you normally do this?"

Michael flashed a smile. "Do what, break the law? Only when my brother and his wife are in danger." He leaned into the car and held out his hand. "Keys."

Dr. Sparrow tossed the keys outside. He spat. "Fuck you."

Michael slammed the door and picked the keys off the ground. He said, "Get in. I'm driving."

"Where are we going?"

"Away from here. Now get in before someone sees us."

•

Michael Candle, you are one crazy son of a bitch. The words repeated in the detective's head as he guided the car out of the alley and into traffic. Everything caught up to him in those moments, the sequence of events replaying in a constant blur behind his eyes, and he realized the gravity of what they'd done.

More words played like a litany through his skull: armed kidnapping, hostage-taking.

He looked in the rearview mirror at Dr. Sparrow. The old man glared at Michael's reflection, his cheeks stained a dark shade of red. His face looked like a giant bruise.

What are you doing? Michael asked himself. He turned his attention back to the road, struggling against the urge to turn the car around or sucker-punch his brother for dragging him into this mess. *Take the old man back to the bookstore. Drop him off. Apologize for the bad prank, and get the hell out of there.*

Despite what he'd witnessed since the previous night, with his brother's inexplicable vanishing acts and the conversation with the weirdo on the phone, he still resisted belief. It was something he'd built up over the years, a requirement for logic that ran deep in his veins, and it was hard to shake. This logic told him they *would* be caught, and they *would* go to jail.

However, there was more to all this than he understood, and this depth undermined his rationale, stirring something within him. It was a fear that there *was* something greater at stake, something deeply rooted in the world which they took for granted. It was something he was sure he would never fully understand. Whatever *it* was made him set aside his fear of breaking the law.

For the moment, all he understood was that his sister-in-law was in trouble, and he'd do whatever was necessary to help his brother get her back.

Michael drove, his path describing a straight line from downtown toward the outskirts of the city, eventually headed toward the countryside. His mind raced. For a few minutes all he could think about was how he had turned the corner and spotted the old man with his gun to Donovan's head. Providence led him to that alleyway—the store was at capacity, and he was one of the many who were denied entrance. He watched from the window, and when the old man retreated to the back, something—a stir in his gut, a prickle at the back of his neck—spurred his feet to action.

The gut feeling. Every gumshoe had one.

Now his gut told him the old man was bad news, and not just because of the gun. There was a cold intensity in his tired eyes: murderous, calculating—the eyes of a sociopath, he suspected. And when he looked up in the rearview again, he was relieved to find the good doctor staring out the window.

Donovan spoke up. "How did you know—"

"I didn't. Just a hunch, is all."

"Well, I'm glad."

Michael glanced over at his brother, then back at the rearview reflection. Dr. Sparrow stared back.

"Are you two faggots or something?"

Michael signaled a turn, guiding the car to the far end of a vacant parking lot. He put the car in park and shut off the engine.

"We're going to sort all of this shit out," he said, pointing to Sparrow. "Starting with you, Dr. Dickhead."

"Don't patronize me," Sparrow said. "I may be old, but I've killed punks like you for less."

"Right." Michael pulled Sparrow's gun from his pocket. He set it beside his own revolver on the dashboard. "Is that why you carry this thing? To threaten your fans?"

"I carry it to keep shits like you from doing what he wants."

Michael shot a glance to his brother. Donovan said nothing, his furrowed brow reminding Michael of their youth. It was "the Donovan look," a sure sign that something was brewing somewhere in that rich expanse of brain matter.

"Dr. Sparrow," Donovan said. He spoke slowly, careful with his words. "Mr. Dullington has my wife."

"How can I say this and avoid euphemism?" Dr. Sparrow chuckled quietly. His voice was dry, hollow. "Ah, yes. You're *fucked*."

•

Donovan stared at the old man for a long while, sizing him up. The doctor's words came as a slap in the face. He'd hoped this man might have some answers, that he might work to help him recover Donna in one piece, but after looking into the man's eyes, he realized it was a facade.

He thought of his wife, her smile engraved in his memory. It was all the motivation he needed.

Donovan plucked Sparrow's gun from the dashboard. He raised it, put his finger on the trigger, and pointed it at the old man's forehead.

"You *will* help me, Dr. Sparrow."

"Or what? You'll kill me?" He snickered. "Your master wouldn't like that very much, would he?"

Joe Hopper's words came bubbling out of a red haze and found their way to Donovan's lips.

"One way or another,' Donovan growled, "you're going back. Donna's life is worth ten of yours."

He paused, cringing as Sparrow ground his teeth together. The old man looked like a rabid dog ready to snap.

"Do you really think he'll let you go?"

"He's kept his word so far."

"So far," Sparrow scoffed. "But Dullington always has an angle. He might let your wife go, but he'll still have you. One way or another, he'll *still have you.*"

Michael shook his head. "This guy's so full of shit."

"Full of shit? You don't even know what you're talking about, Mikey. You're not exactly Dullington's type. You haven't been there. You haven't see the things—" Sparrow locked eyes with Donovan. He slowly nodded. "But *you* know what I'm talking about. You *have* been there."

Donovan looked away, his cheeks flushed with heat. He tried not to think about the Monochrome, its emptiness, the lifeless drone humming through the very air, or the pale things that inhabited it. A chill worked its way down the back of his neck.

Sparrow propped his elbow against the window. "You aren't the first. You won't be the last. His game's been going on for a very long time."

"Why does he want you?"

"Because," Sparrow twirled his fingers, "I'm the one who

got away. The rest of them, they're just there in the 'chrome to be sucked dry. You, your brother, everyone on this planet—you're all cattle. Once you go over for good, you belong to him." The old man paused, thinking. "What do you do for a living?"

Donovan lowered the weapon. "I work for an identity theft monitoring service. Sales department."

"So you're a salesman? Oh my." Sparrow put his head back and let out a hearty laugh. Donovan glared. "I can't imagine a more mediocre job. No wonder you're flickering. Frankly, I'm surprised everyone in your workplace hasn't vanished."

"That's beside the point." Donovan muttered.

"Ah, so it is," Sparrow grinned. He took off his glasses and cleaned them with his handkerchief. "Dullington wanted me to take his place. I used to be just like you, living an empty life. Then one day I woke up and found I was disappearing. And I let it happen, too. I started seeing little things on people's shoulders, whispering for them to forget me, and then I started seeing the bigger ones—the Yawning, he calls them. Not long after that, I found myself lost in a gray haze." He kept running the lenses through his handkerchief, wiping them with a circular motion. "Aleister Dullington made himself known to me. He said, 'I will set you apart from the others, Mr. Sparrow. I will deliver you unto banality.'"

Sparrow squeezed so hard the lenses cracked. One of them fell from its frame.

"I didn't like the prospect of an eternity in that gray hell, so I found a way out."

Donovan leaned forward, caught up in the doctor's reverie. "How?"

"Mediocrity is a fickle thing. Anything can be mediocre. I surmised that whatever boring thing led me to the Monochrome could be counteracted by an equal and opposite excitement."

Michael muttered under his breath and shook his head. Donovan shot him an annoyed glance but said nothing. Sparrow went on:

"Being one of the Missing means being on the brink of starvation. There's nothing tangible in the Monochrome. No food, no water. Dullington let us into the Spectrum once a day to feed, and our time there was limited to scrounging for table scraps, rummaging through dumpsters, living like transients." Sparrow put down his broken glasses. He picked up the cracked lens and examined it. "I figured an event of drastic proportions could propel me out of the Monochrome just long enough to weaken its pull. I needed to reach a kind of escape velocity, if you will."

Donovan's throat clicked when he swallowed. The car's enclosed space suddenly felt very small.

"What did you do?"

Sparrow held up the lens with both hands. "He let us into the Spectrum in pairs, one to watch the other. If one misbehaved, both would suffer punishment. My partner was a man called Smith, a sad sack of shit who clung to some perverse hope that things might change one day. I knew better. I knew change wouldn't come; it had to be pursued and taken with force." He snapped the lens in half. It broke in two, jagged pieces. Small shards fell to the seat. "So I took matters into my hands. I murdered the poor bastard. It was enough to get me out of there."

The doctor's macabre confession did not startle Donovan, he'd already witnessed more than enough of the man's true character to be anything other than sickened. Phantom fingers curled around his stomach and pulled, causing him to flicker for a moment. Sparrow remained in full clarity as the car faded and colors bled from the world.

When it stopped, Donovan caught the old man's eye. "But you're still flickering. If you're flickering, how come people can see you?"

"It's all a matter of negative space."

Michael grunted. "Negative space?"

"Yes," Sparrow sighed, "It is a matter of perception. The odds are you've seen one of the other Missing without even knowing it." He traced his finger along the edge of the lens shard. "Imagine a painting of a vase. At a glance, you see the vase, but if you were to look closer, you might see a face on either side. Both images are visible, but you only see one at a time."

"But what about those—" Michael snapped his fingers, searching for the right word. Sparrow finished for him.

"Cretins. They act as a veil, covering up the faces. They exist so you only see the vase. And in the odd chance you're lucky enough to perceive the faces, they ensure you won't remember it."

"That doesn't answer my question," Donovan said.

Sparrow grinned. "A person can weaken their chain to the Monochrome, but they can't break it. Once it's in place, it's there to stay. The weaker it is, the more others are able to see. Even his Cretins can't interfere. In my case, the chain is weak enough that others can see the faces for the vase."

Donovan smirked. "Sounds like you're living on borrowed time."

The sly humor left Sparrow's face. He looked away. "I've taken great pains to keep myself at a distance, correcting where I went wrong. I went back to school, I excelled, I wrote my book and found success, fame. Constantly changing, keeping track of any possible routines, sleeping on the floor once or twice to break the cycle of sleeping in a bed—you'll do anything to keep your head above water when you're drowning." Sparrow looked back at Donovan for a moment, sizing him up. "You're going to wind up just as I did if you don't change your ways. Everyone does."

"Everyone?"

"Poor saps who are tethered to the other side. He's used some of them, sending them after me for the better part of ten years, to do exactly what you're doing now. All of them have something to lose, all are given the promise of freedom if they succeed." A wry grin formed across his face. "You're no different. You're just sinking to new lows to save your own skin."

His words struck Donovan with jarring force. In his struggle to rescue Donna, he'd become no different than George Guffin by kidnapping this man. *But Donna's life depends on it*, he thought.

"All you had to do was talk to me," he whispered. "I didn't want to force you."

"Oh, please." Sparrow rolled his eyes. "You know damn well I wouldn't have come with you, regardless of whatever sob-story you tried to sell me."

Donovan closed his eyes and took a breath. Joe Hopper's voice spoke up within the darkness of his head, and Donovan didn't like what he had to say. *Up against a wall, boss, and you're damned either way. But the old codger's got a point—sometimes you can't wait for change to come. You have to make it yourself.*

He thought of Donna again, and he realized he'd already made up his mind long before encountering this vile excuse of a man.

"I told Dullington I'd bring you to him, and that's what I intend to do."

"Your weakness is beneath you. Even if you get her back, it won't change the fact that you'll soon be his. Too many people refuse to change, and you're just like them, another tick on Dullington's fucking chalkboard." His words ran together in a guttural deluge of rage. "*You'll end up right back there with me in the end, and I'll make sure you regret it every fucking day.*"

Sparrow took the broken lens and lunged forward. Donovan reacted without thinking, lifting his hand to block the attack, crying out as the lens cut a gash across his palm. Sparrow recoiled, growling incomprehensible words as he pulled back for another slash—

Michael brought down the butt of his revolver against Sparrow's head. It connected with a dull thud, and Donovan watched lights go out in the old man's eyes. The glass shard slipped from his fingers and fell to the floor. Sparrow slumped back into the seat with a faint groan. A thin line of blood trickled from his silver temple.

"You okay?"

Donovan put pressure on his wound to slow the bleeding. "Yeah."

He was distant, his mind lost in a mental replay of the doctor's words. He wondered if he would be stuck living a life transparent forever, flickering in and out of existence while fading into complete obscurity. Thinking back, he realized it was all he'd done for the last nine years. Working at Identinel had drained the last ounce of life from his body. Now he was just a drone, and he had nothing to show for his life because he hadn't done anything with it.

"So what now?"

"Now I guess we—"

Donovan's cell phone vibrated in his pocket. A moment later, Michael's cell phone rang. Outside, a row of old pay phones rang in succession, forming a melody of buzzing notes.

Michael shook his head, amazed. "I think it's for you."

"I think you might be right." Donovan pulled the dead cell phone from his pocket, flipped it open, and answered.

•

"You impress me more with each passing moment, Mr. Candle. I applaud you."

"I have him. What do you want me to do with him?"

The static in the line rose and fell, echoing laughter. "Listen to yourself. You kidnap one man, and now you are ready to take on the world."

Donovan clenched his teeth. "I'm not proud of what I had to do."

"Do not pity him, Mr. Candle. He is not as innocent as he makes himself out to be. I assure you, given the opportunity he would do the same to you without a second thought."

He looked back at the unconscious man, remembering the hatred in Sparrow's eyes.

"I just want my wife back, Dullington."

"And so you shall have her, in time."

Donovan shook so hard he almost dropped the phone. He balled his free hand into a tight fist. The anger came from a deep place, fueled by his fatigue and heartache.

"I have your goddamn puppet," he growled. "Now just give her back. She's all I want. I've done what you've asked."

"Calm yourself, Mr. Candle. You are correct in your statement—you have done everything I have asked of you, and you will be rewarded."

He closed his eyes for a moment and cleared his head. He told himself to focus, to suck it up and suffer the last few strides to the finish line. An image of Donna's smiling face rekindled the dying fire within. Donovan opened his eyes and looked outside.

"Where do you want us to take him?"

"Are you familiar with the Yellow Line?"

Donovan thought for a moment. "The subway?"

"Correct. It is not in use anymore. I prefer it due to its level of discretion." Dullington paused, allowing a hiss of static to fill the space. "You might say it also possesses a certain liminal quality. Appropriate, I think."

"Anything else?"

"I believe that is all, Mr. Candle. My associates will be waiting for you at the entrance."

A rush of white noise filled his ear before the click. Donovan stared at the phone's blank screen. It was dead again.

"Well?"

He looked up at his brother. "She's at the subway."

"The subway?" Michael frowned. "Which one?"

"The Yellow Line."

"Christ. It's been out of service for years."

"I know. Can you get us there?"

Michael started the car and let its engine answer for him. He turned around in the parking lot and entered traffic.

"Why the subway?" he asked. "Of all the places . . ."

Donovan shrugged, watching as they returned to the city. *A subway*, he thought, *is in a constant state of transition. It's always between two points. Always liminal.*

Liminal. That word again. He decided he would be happy if he could live the rest of his life without hearing that word.

Dr. Sparrow stirred, whimpering quietly to himself. Donovan looked back at the old man and thought about his words. *You'll end up right back there with me in the end. Too many people refuse to change.* It occurred to him that this was his only chance. Getting Donna back from Dullington was his first priority, but he'd let her down if he didn't make it through this, too. He'd cheated her enough over the years. It was time to atone and make things up to her.

Michael was about to turn onto the bypass and take the shorter route when Donovan asked him not to.

"Why? This is faster."

"Trust me."

"All right," Michael said, shrugging. He guided the car out of the turn-lane and moved on toward the city.

It was the opposite of what Donovan would've done, and that was precisely the point. For the first time since the flickering began, he felt a strange sense of peace come over him. It felt right, doing what he was doing, even if it scared him to death.

His fear was a simple fear of the unknown. For the first time in his life, Donovan Candle learned to accept that fear. He embraced it.

As they drove on through the city, Donovan made a silent commitment to Donna, to himself. From now on, he would choose to take the path less traveled. A life transparent was not one he wanted to live, and he would do everything he could to prove Dr. Sparrow wrong.

-11-
A STATE OF LOVE AND LIMINALITY

M‌OVEMENT, AND FOOTSTEPS. Donna opened her eyes just as a dark shape knelt beside her. Her heart skipped a couple of beats.

"Mrs. Candle?"

It was Alice. Donna looked up at her, tried to make out her face. Firelight cast dancing shadows upon the wall of the room, giving the young woman's cheeks a faint, orange outline that traced a smile in the dark.

Donna tried to sit up, wincing as her limbs woke in agony. Alice put a hand behind Donna's neck to help.

"He's coming," Alice said, and for the first time in a day, Donna broke her vow of silence. Her voice cracked.

"Donnie?"

There was a quick tearing sound, and Donna discovered she could move her legs again. Alice helped her to her feet.

"We're moving you to the meeting place. You'll see him very soon."

•

"Is that it?"

Michael brought the car to a stop alongside a building that used to house a small department store. Its display windows were shattered and boarded up. Graffiti artists had claimed those boards as their own, marking them with bright neon colors and insignias.

Across the street was an entrance ramp. A sign stood beside it, its letters faded, featuring a yellow circle in its center.

"That looks like the place," Donovan said, surveying their bleak surroundings. Since construction of the highway bypass over thirty years ago, this previously bustling portion of town had dwindled, dried up, and finally died. Most of the city's crimes were committed in the South district, and even the cops were hesitant to venture its cracked, transient-ridden streets after dark. Donovan and Michael had the advantage of an overcast afternoon sky, but not much else.

Michael shut off the engine and looked at Donovan.

"Do we know what we're doing?"

A cold tendril snaked its way around his gut. "No, Mike, I don't think we do."

Michael checked both guns, then handed his brother the revolver. Donovan took it with reservation, afraid to put his finger anywhere near the trigger. He'd decided in the last 24 hours that he didn't like guns very much.

"When did you get this thing?"

Michael shrugged. "A few years ago. Figured it might come in handy."

"Has it?"

"You tell me." They exchanged nervous smiles. Dr. Sparrow mumbled in his sleep.

Donovan looked back at the old man, noting his helplessness, and his stomach lurched. A hint of bile rose in the back of his throat. *Can I do this?* The answer came, as it always did, from Joe Hopper: *Sure you can, boss. What other choice do you have? Now get to it.*

"I guess we should wake up Sleeping Beauty."

They got out of the car. Michael opened the passenger door.

"Hey, doc." He slapped Sparrow's cheeks. "Rise and shine."

Dr. Sparrow's eyes opened into narrow slits. He winced as he sat up, touching a hand to his forehead. He looked at the brothers for a moment, then at his surroundings. Everything came back to him.

"You hit me."

"I did." Michael took him by the arm. "Get out of the car."

Donovan turned his attention to the subway entrance across the street. The flickering overcame him, revealing a street teeming with Cretins and Yawning. The creatures separated, forming a path toward the stairs. Donna was down there in the dark. His heart began to pound.

When the Spectrum's colors bled their way into reality, Donovan turned to find Dr. Sparrow staring at him.

"It won't be long," he snickered. "You're going to fade right into oblivion."

Donovan gripped the revolver. "We'll see about that."

They crossed the street in a single-file line. Donovan led the way, while Michael took up the rear. He pushed the barrel of his gun into the small of Dr. Sparrow's back.

A gate barred their entrance at the bottom of the stairs. Donovan pulled on it, but it did not budge. A padlock was affixed to the handle from the inside.

No. He gripped the bars and pulled as hard as he could. *Not now,* he thought. *I'm so close.*

He cursed as he shook the bars, sending an echo down into the darkness beyond. His legs weakened and he collapsed to his knees, his fingers still wrapped around the bars.

Sparrow chuckled. It rose slowly within his tiny frame, increasing in volume, transforming into a cruel, maniacal cackling that caught Donovan off guard. Donovan glared up at him. A new strength found its way to his legs. He was on his feet and at the old man's throat within seconds, but Michael was faster. He held his brother back.

"Don't."

Donovan clutched at Sparrow's collar. For a brief moment there was fear in the old man's eyes, but it quickly faded. He smiled.

"Listen to him, Donovan. If Dullington wants me alive, you'd do well to mind him."

Donovan stepped back. He leaned against the concrete wall,

took a breath, and ran his hands through his hair.

What would Joe Hopper do? he thought. *What would I do?*

He looked at the gate and its padlock, then remembered his pistol. Michael connected the dots just as Donovan moved toward the bars.

"If you're thinking about shooting the lock, I wouldn't do it."

Donovan looked back at his brother. "Why not? I've seen it—"

"In movies. So have I. But if you shoot that lock, all you'll do is damage it, and then no one's getting it open."

He looked down at the lock. *So much for that idea.*

"Do you know how to pick locks?"

Michael shook his head. "Maybe there's another entrance. Keep an eye on him—I'll be right back."

"Mike—"

But Michael was already halfway up the steps. When he reached street level, he looked down at Donovan and winked, though the gesture did little to alleviate the panic welling up inside him. After all he'd gone through to get to this point, Donovan could not help but feel defeated. Doubt crept into his thoughts. Had Dullington set him up to fail? Did he even intend to follow through with his part of the deal?

The gray sight returned, painting the world in Monochrome shades. Dr. Sparrow shone through, a malignant beacon in an otherwise unremarkable landscape. When he flickered back, Donovan found the good doctor watching him.

Donovan sat on the steps. He kept the revolver in plain sight to ensure there were no illusions between them. He might not be able to kill Sparrow, but he realized he would have no problem putting a bullet in the man's leg.

"It's happening," Sparrow said, "and it's only going to get worse." He nodded to the gate. "And do you think he'll really give back your wife? Once he gets what he wants, he'll fuck you over just like the rest of them."

The rest of them. Donovan let the doctor's words sink in. He remembered Sparrow's analogy about negative spaces. How many times had he given a homeless person more than a hurried glance? There were invisible men and women inhabiting every part of the city, in every part of the country, and no one acknowledged them. How many of them were Dullington's slaves?

The prospect of millions lost in the Monochrome terrified him.

"Are there really others?"

Sparrow rested his head against the wall and closed his eyes. "More than you could ever imagine. People like you, with meaningless lives, born with no real purpose, and obscured by their own mediocrity."

"Is that why you wrote your book?"

Dr. Sparrow looked down at him. He seemed genuinely surprised. "Why do you think I wrote my book?"

"I'd like to believe you wanted to help people. To warn them."

Sparrow scoffed. "I don't *care* about people. I don't *care* about you. The book is eighty thousand words of bullshit wrapped in a neat package and marketed to people who think they want to better their lives. *Help* people? Please." He shook his head. "People are insects. They don't give a shit. They don't want to better themselves. They only want to eat, fuck, and watch reality television."

Donovan frowned. "I'm not like that."

"And I don't believe you. You wouldn't be here if that were true."

He thought about this. *I just want to support myself and my wife. Maybe a child some day, too.* Days before, if asked, Donovan would have said he wanted life with all its material perks. He would've wanted that promotion at his job, which in the scheme of things meant only a few more pennies on the hour. And what good would that do? He would just use it as a reason to strive for even more he couldn't have. Donna was right: it was never enough for him.

Donovan realized these things weren't all he wanted out of life. Not really. A flash of Donna's smiling face in his mind confirmed what he already knew.

"I just want to be happy," he whispered.

"Ah, happiness," Sparrow said. "Society raises you to believe it's attainable. They show you their view of what happiness is, and then they set you free to find your own. 'Go, find happiness.' It's the greatest con of all."

"Con?"

"Of course. I figured a man of your apparent intelligence would recognize that. It's a rigged game, kid. The happiness we're taught to buy doesn't exist. We're all running in place trying to snatch the carrot dangling out of reach. People sacrifice their lives for something they can never have. Some of them—the worst of them—end up like us." He rubbed absently at the wound on his forehead. "Tell me, how long have you been a salesman?"

Donovan felt the heat of embarrassment, but found no reason to run from the truth any longer. There was no point in lying to himself or Sparrow.

"Nine years," he said. "Nine long, fruitless years."

"And here you are. I saw you flickering. It's how you're going to pay for your greatest crime."

"What are you talking about? What crime?"

"A crime against your own humanity. You've squandered your life by not reaching your own potential as a human being. That's what brought me to the Monochrome, and that's what will inevitably happen to you. Yours has become a life transparent."

Donovan smirked. "Is that a line out of your book?"

"No." Sparrow's eyes narrowed. "It's not."

Footsteps above broke the tension between them. Michael Candle jogged down the steps and caught his breath.

"I found another entrance," he said, "but it was locked up, too."

Donovan's heart sank. He looked back at the gate, wishing he had a crowbar or—

A beam of light traced across the wall, revealing markings of graffiti and cracks in the concrete. The light bobbed up and down, growing brighter as it neared. Donovan rose to his feet and took a step toward the gate.

"What the hell is that?" Michael asked, but Donovan said nothing. He and Sparrow looked into the darkness beyond the bars. A pale circle of light came into view, bobbing its way toward them.

"Donovan Candle?" asked a voice. It was weak, quiet. At first Donovan wasn't sure if he should answer. When the voice called out to him again, he walked to the gate and spoke.

"Y-Yes," he said. "I'm here."

A young man stepped forward, squinting into the daylight. He held a flashlight in his hand.

Donovan got a good look at him. He was dressed in a tattered button-down dress shirt and torn khakis. Half of a tie hung from his neck. He looked, in all ways, like absolute hell, and that's when Donovan realized he was staring at one of Dullington's casualties.

•

"Who are you?"

"Name's Joel."

Donovan glanced at his brother, who remained on the steps. He shrugged.

"Joel. Do you know why we're here?"

"Oh yes," he said. "Mr. Dullington told us to expect you. He said you'd be nearby, and here you are." He shifted his gaze over Donovan's shoulder, toward the old man. "Is this Dr. Sparrow?"

Sparrow glared at him. Joel offered a weak smile and looked back at Donovan.

"Very good," he said, producing a key from his pocket. "I'll let you through."

"Where is my wife?" His words sounded rushed, more panicked than Donovan expected, and he tried to get a grip on himself.

Joel ignored his urgency. He opened the padlock and pushed open the gate. It swung back with a shrill cry of agony that echoed down into the dark. He looked back at the trio and pointed his flashlight at the shadows.

"This way."

Donovan hesitated, then took a breath and entered. The air was stale, musty. *This must be what a tomb smells like*, he thought, turning back to face the opening. Michael lowered the handgun and pushed it against Sparrow's back.

"Easy does it, old timer."

Sparrow waited at the threshold, glaring into the darkness. Beads of sweat dotted his forehead, and there was slight tremble in his chin. He caught Donovan's eye just before stepping into the darkness.

"This is going to haunt you, Donovan Candle. *I'm* going to haunt you." Sparrow's words echoed down the stairwell. Donovan thought about responding, but the words faltered on his tongue.

Once Michael was inside, Joel closed the gate and engaged the padlock. He pointed the flashlight at Sparrow, forcing the old man to back away and squint.

"I've heard much about you, Dr. Sparrow. The master said you might try to run."

Sparrow flashed a smile. "Your master was right."

He moved fast, shoving his elbow into Michael's gut. Donovan was still looking down into the darkened stairwell, and when he looked back at the commotion he was blinded by daylight pouring across the threshold.

Michael's gun clattered on the floor. Sparrow snatched it up, spun on his heels, and was about to fire at the young man, but Michael was faster. He growled, grabbing the old man's arm just as the gun went off. The shot filled the cavern, amplifying into a small explosion that made Donovan's ears ring.

"*I won't go back!*" Sparrow screamed. He used his free arm to claw at Michael's face as the two men struggled into the shadows. Donovan lifted the revolver, but he couldn't find a clean shot. Not that it would have made a difference—his heart was pounding like a jackhammer, and his hands shook along with it.

Joel pointed the light into the darkness of the shrouded tunnel, searching for the two men. They could be heard scuffling, but the beam of light failed to reveal them. Donovan muttered under his breath and stepped into the dark. Joel followed, lighting the way.

Finally, after a moment of searching, they heard Michael shout. They found him at the next landing. He knelt on the ground, a hand to his jaw.

"The son of a bitch clocked me."

Donovan did not waste any time. He snatched the flashlight from Joel's hands and descended the steps two at a time. Michael called out to him, but he did not stop. His body moved with a will all its own.

The beam danced across the walls, compounding his confusion and panic. *Find him*, his mind screamed. If Sparrow got away, Donna was done for. That thought raced laps across his brain as he moved down to the subway terminal.

The stairwell finally opened up into a larger cavern littered with garbage and other human detritus: broken furniture, bags of trash, food wrappers, discarded cans. A fire in an old refuse barrel illuminated the room, casting dancing shadows across its walls. Donovan concentrated his flashlight along the floor, following the beam of light to a token booth, its windows shattered and door smeared with years of grime. The smell of the place made his head swim. It stank of dried waste, and he wondered how long it had been since the transients—the Missing—had made this place their home.

There came a scream out of the dark, followed by a gunshot. It gave Donovan a start, his chest thumping with panic. Was it a woman's scream? A lump formed in his throat. He fought back a bout of nausea.

Keep your head straight, boss. You don't know if it's her.

There were more shouts now, some of them belonging to his brother and the young man he'd left in the stairway. Others came from somewhere further ahead, distorted and impossible to decipher. *Donna*, he thought. *She's here. She's close.*

And she'll be dead if you don't find that old bastard.

He sucked in his breath and leapt over the turnstiles.

•

The stairwell gave way to the boarding platform. More barrels illuminated the wide room with dancing shadows that played tricks on Donovan's eyes. The walls seemed to move with varying shapes. The whole room glowed a sinister orange hue, reminding him of a Halloween bonfire he attended as a child.

In the center of the platform, between two columns, stood a crowd of people. Donovan couldn't tell how many there were. They seemed to wait, their attention focused on something at the edge of the platform. Some of the people, he saw, were covered in grime, their skin mottled with an ashy-colored pox. The smell here was even worse, and Donovan had to suppress the urge to vomit.

"*Put it down,*" a woman screamed. She sounded young. There were mumbles of concern and dissent among the group. Off in the corner, Donovan glanced at a pair of men kneeling over the body of a woman. He panicked for a moment, fearing it might be his wife, but her voice over the crowd caught his attention.

"Mister, please, you don't have to do this—"

"Shut up, bitch."

Donovan froze. *No*, he thought. He gripped the revolver and cocked back the hammer like he'd seen on TV. It clicked. A woman in the crowd turned, saw him standing there, then pointed him out to the man next to her. They watched Donovan force his way through the crowd toward the pair at the edge of the platform.

Dr. Albert Sparrow stood with an arm wrapped around Donna's neck. She was frozen with fear, her arms limp at her sides like a ragdoll. Tears streamed down her face.

Sparrow pressed the gun against her temple. He saw Donovan at the entrance. He did not smile.

"I'm not going back," he said. "I don't know if I made that clear enough yet, but I think I've got your attention now. Drop the gun."

Michael and Joel finally caught up to him. They ran down the stairs and halted at the opening. Donovan heard his brother mutter "Shit" under his breath.

"You don't have to do this," Donovan began. His mouth was suddenly very dry, and the revolver felt like a lead weight in his hand.

"Drop the gun."

Donovan looked into Donna's eyes. He wanted to cross the gap, take her in his arms, and hold her. He wanted to tell her how sorry he was—but he couldn't. He glared at Sparrow as he placed the gun on the floor. Joe Hopper's words came to him, except they weren't really Hopper's at all. They were Donovan's, and the sound of them on his lips filled him with an unsteady terror.

"If you hurt her," he said, "*I will haunt you.*"

Sparrow flashed a smile, taking the gun away from Donna's head for a moment. "Your wife and I are going to walk out of here, Don, and we're going to take the car. You'll find her dumped on the side of the road somewhere. What you do now determines whether or not she'll still be breathing when you do."

Anger welled up within Donovan, climbing from his gut all the way to his head. His vision reddened. For a moment, he forgot about everything else. He forgot about the flickering, about his brother and the others, about his own measly existence. In that quiet span of seconds, Donovan saw only the old man and his wife. A cold weight coiled around his stomach, transforming into fingers that gripped his torso, lightly pulling him out of the Spectrum.

He looked at Donna. "I love you," he said. Donovan breathed deeply as he took a step toward Sparrow. The old man pointed the gun at him just as the world shifted. Shadows gave way to a graying haze that filled the room like thick smoke. The cracked and grimy tile floor vanished, revealing a blank panel. The others shone through in clarity. He could see their features. *Liminal people*, he thought.

Sparrow was there, too, holding Donna's darkened silhouette.

Donovan crossed the gap and charged into the doctor. The grays faded, filling in the blanks of the room with the spotted orange glow of fire in the shadows. Sparrow let go of Donna as the two of them tumbled off the platform and onto the old tracks.

The impact drove the air from Donovan's lungs, but it did little to quell the fire burning within him. He drove his knee into Sparrow's groin, eliciting a hoarse cry from the doctor. His gnarled fingers searched the ground around them, fumbling for the gun, but it was not within reach.

Donovan clutched Sparrow's throat. He balled his other hand into a fist, letting his rage take over. All Donovan could hear was the smack of his knuckles against the old man's face. All he could see was the image of Sparrow's gun to Donna's head. After coming all this way and compromising his own values, Donovan would not let anything happen to her, and certainly not at the hands of this man.

The room shifted again, colors becoming gray. The empty drone of the Monochrome took over. Donovan thrust himself off the doctor, panting. Blood dripped off his swollen knuckles, spotting the floor beneath him. In a few seconds, the dark red splotches vanished, erased by this pale reality.

He looked up. The Missing stood at the edge of the platform, watching.

Is that it? he wondered. *Have I flickered out?*

"Not quite, Mr. Candle."

Dullington's voice sounded as if from everywhere, each syllable accompanied by a tremor running through the very fabric of reality. Cretins emerged from the tunnels, spilling over one another, chattering incessantly. They stopped short of Donovan and Sparrow, climbing atop one another to form a column of white, squirming bodies. Aleister Dullington's features took shape.

He looked down at Sparrow. The old man faded in and out of the gray haze, his body shimmering with color.

"Contrary to what Albert Sparrow told you, Mr. Candle, I am a being of my word."

"No," Sparrow groaned. Dullington ignored him. He set his black eyes upon Donovan.

"I am in your debt. You have done what no one else could do, and all in the name of love."

"So that's it, then?" Donovan crawled backward, resting against the side of the platform. "You'll let my wife go?"

"Indeed I will, Mr. Candle. I must confess, under normal circumstances I would keep you here, and I still may." A hint of a smile spread across Dullington's face. "But that is up to you."

"What do you mean?"

"Your second chance, Mr. Candle. It *is* a second chance, and it *is* yours. Not many are granted one, but when they do it is earned." Dullington's voice degraded into a slow growl. "Albert Sparrow cheated his way to it." He looked up at the others standing on the edge of the platform. "Take him away. He will flicker out in time."

Albert Sparrow groaned, his voice distorted by the gravity of the Monochrome. Donovan watched the good doctor flicker back to the Spectrum. He felt shame for what he'd done, leaving the man to this fate—but he had no other choice.

"What's going to happen to him?"

"I have plans for him, but he is no longer your concern, Mr. Candle. Do you remember what I asked you yesterday?"

Donovan did remember. "I do."

"Good. Therein lies the way to your second chance. Consider it a life pitch."

"A life pitch?"

Dullington nodded. "Define yourself, Mr. Candle. It is the only way you will truly stop the flickering. If you do not do this, you *will* see me again, and I am not in the business of granting third chances."

The room shifted before Donovan had a chance to respond. He found himself sitting in the darkness of the subway tunnel. Dr. Sparrow was gone.

•

"Donnie?"

He found new strength at the sound of Donna's voice. He pulled himself onto the platform. A group of the Missing watched him in quiet awe. Donna pushed her way through the crowd and threw her arms around him. He held her tight, eyes closed, relishing the moment, then pulled back and kissed her. It was a kiss of desperation and love, seeming to stop time.

When he pulled away, she gasped and smiled. Tears welled up in her eyes.

"I'm so sorry."

"This isn't your fault," he said, fighting back his own tears. "This isn't your fault at all."

A young woman approached them. Donovan gave her a curious glance as recognition teased his mind. He'd seen her before, somewhere. Donna looked over at her, offering a weak smile.

"Mrs. Candle," the woman said, "I'm sorry all of this happened to you. And you, too, Donovan."

"Do I know you?" he asked.

Alice nodded. He couldn't tell if she was smiling or frowning—the shifting shadows cast by the firelight made it hard to see.

"You did, once. We worked in the same department at Identinel."

"What's your name?"

"Alice Walenta."

The name rushed out of the depths of his mind with the velocity of a bullet. He knew her face, and he knew her name, but not from the job. That connection was dead to him, but the rest—

The radio ads, he thought. *The newspaper ads, too.* "Her name is Alice Walenta. She is 5'9", roughly 150 lbs, and has long, black hair." She fit the description, and he knew without a doubt that this was her. She belonged to Dullington now, another casualty of the flickering. George Guffin's panicked words came rushing back: "*Some forget about us and others don't.*"

"The last time I saw you, Don Candle, you had a Cretin on your shoulder. You never even knew I was gone. Do you still work for that hideous company?"

He didn't know what to say to her. For the life of him, he could not remember her at all from the workplace. There was a hazy spot in his memory, like a square cut away from canvas. How many others had he known and forgotten? The implications of the question chilled him.

Michael Candle approached them. He looked confused, and more frightened than he would ever admit.

"Are you two okay?"

"Yeah," Donovan said, giving Donna a squeeze. "I think so."

"Good." Michael nodded. "Now can we get the hell out of here?"

They all agreed it was time to return home. Alice got the key from Joel and led them back the way they came, through the suffocating darkness, up the stairs toward the locked gate. The daylight stung their eyes. Alice kept her head down while she opened the lock.

Michael bounded up the steps to the sidewalk. As Donovan helped his wife across the threshold, he took a breath, relishing the fresh air. Alice waited at the gate, squinting up to the sky. She, too, breathed in the air. It brought a smile to her face.

Donovan took to the stairs, but Donna paused to look back.

"What's wrong?"

Donna ignored him. "Alice," she said. "Come with us. I don't know what's happened, but maybe we can help you?"

Alice stepped back into the shadows. She closed the gate and engaged the padlock.

"I'm sorry, Mrs. Candle. It doesn't work like that." There were tears in the young woman's eyes. She blinked them away. "This is my place now, and it wouldn't matter if I went with you. Sooner or later, you would forget about me."

Donna beckoned to the woman beyond the gate, but Alice had vanished into the shadows. Donna looked at her husband, confused, and took her first, reluctant step toward freedom.

When they reached the top, Donovan stopped to look down at the gate. He thought about what Alice said, measuring the weight of her words. He understood them and their heavy implications, and when he looked back at his wife, he realized what he had to do.

Donovan put his back to the threshold and wrapped an arm around Donna.

"Come on," he said. "Let's go home."

-EPILOGUE-
LIFE PITCH

Donovan Candle's alarm went off precisely at 6:30 Monday morning. He stirred in his sleep, rolled over and snuggled his wife, who promptly nudged him. He opened his eyes and stared at the ceiling. The alarm blared. Memories of the weekend came tumbling upward from a shallow grave, threatening to drag him down into its hole.

Worse than the denizens of the Monochrome were the prospects of returning to an empty job, an empty routine. An empty life.

Timothy Butler and the Tammys didn't help matters, either.

"Don," his wife groaned. He smiled, reached over, and turned off the alarm. Donna rolled over, burying her face into his chest.

His thoughts returned to Saturday night, after they retrieved his car and left Sparrow's rental in the parking garage. They stayed at Michael's place that night, mindful enough not to wake him as they made love well into the dawn. When they arrived home Sunday morning, Donovan made his wife wait in the car while he collected the remains of Mr. Precious Paws. He buried the feline in the backyard, marking the grave with his food dish. They spent the rest of the day cleaning the kitchen.

Three times that day, Donovan saw the Monochrome side of his own home. Seeing Donna reduced to a dark, transparent ghost left him with a chill that would not relent. After all he'd gone through it almost didn't seem real, like a dream from which he'd not yet awakened. He wanted it all to be a dream, but the flickering reminded him this was not the case. As he stared toward the ceiling, the room's color drained away. It lasted only a matter of seconds, but it was enough to reassure him this was far from over.

He recalled Dullington's task.

Ain't no better time than today, hoss. Get to it.

Sooner or later he would have to confront the demons that had condemned him for so many years. Today, he realized, would be that day.

Donna lay with her eyes closed. He brushed the hair out of her face. She was so beautiful. He'd gone through hell to get her back, digging to depths of himself he didn't care to know, and it had been worth every moment—but there was still one more life that needed saving.

Her eyes fluttered open. She smiled.

"Good morning," she whispered.

"Hi." He tucked a strand of hair behind her ear. "I need to talk to you about something."

"Mmm, about what?"

The words were there on his tongue. They'd been there ever since Tuesday morning, but other matters had stolen his attention. Even then, he realized, he wouldn't have meant them. Not like now. Now he knew the error of his ways, and he owed her an apology.

Donovan leaned over and kissed her forehead.

"I'm sorry about our fight Monday evening. It was stupid, and you were right all along. It's not about the money."

He felt the heat of tears in his eyes, and tried his best to hold them back. The look on Donna's face told him he wasn't doing a very good job.

"And when I came home the next day, and you weren't there, I thought I'd lost you forever. That I'd driven you away, and in some ways, I think I did. But I want you to know that I'm going to change all that. Today. Because I love you, because I owe it to you, and because . . ." *Because if I don't, I'll disappear forever.* The words hung on his lips, and he wanted to voice them, but he couldn't bring himself to do so. "Just because."

Donna smiled, wiping a tear from his cheek.

"We'll be okay, Donnie. We've seen worse before, and we survived. And if we can survive this, I'd say we're damn near invincible."

"I love you," he said.

She smiled. "And I love you."

They kissed. He'd spent over twenty-four hours without her, and it caused him more agony than he'd ever known before. In some ways, losing her proved his love for her, and now that she was back, he intended to embrace her company for as long as he could. The thought of spending the day away from her while he toiled for nine hours in his cubicle sickened him.

"So, Mrs. Candle," he said. "Would you like to accompany me on a trip to the shore?"

Donna smiled, opened her mouth to speak, but recoiled with a jolt. She cringed for a moment, putting her fingers to her temples.

"Sorry," she gasped. "It's this damn migraine. What were you saying?"

But Donovan didn't respond. He saw all he needed to see in a brief flash of gray. There was a Cretin on her shoulder, its head pointed toward her ear. Alice Walenta's words echoed in his head: *Sooner or later, you would forget about me.*

When the room regained its color, he found Donna staring at him.

"Honey, are you okay?"

"Yeah," Donovan croaked. "I'm fine."

"You're very pale." She put her hand to his forehead. "Doesn't feel like you're running a fever, though. What were you going to say a few seconds ago?"

He looked at her for a moment, contemplating what to say. What could he say? And would it even matter? She could still see him, but what about that evening after work? These questions raced through his head. He had to confront Dullington's challenge, and soon, or else all he'd done would be for nothing. *Define yourself, Mr. Candle.* It was a simple imperative, and yet so daunting. Where could he possibly begin?

Donna looked at the clock. "You're going to be late for work."

The answer came to him. He smiled, kissed her, and scrambled out of bed.

•

He left for work, skipping the bypass and taking side-streets all the way across the city. Along the way he listened to the local rock station instead of his usual talk radio, cranking it as loud as the car's tiny stereo could manage. His windows and rearview mirror rattled with each bass drum beat. Whenever he came to a stop, pedestrians would turn their heads and stare. He imagined he looked goofy, blaring this raucous music from the meager speakers of his four-door sedan, but he didn't care. He would use his second chance and beat the flickering.

The gray sight happened only once during his drive, just as he neared his destination. He saw specters walking along the sidewalks. Some of them had Cretins on their shoulders. It comforted him to see that some did not.

When he neared his office building, he felt that unsteady pull at his stomach. It was fleeting. He drove past the Identinel offices and further into the city, ever mindful to take side streets just as he'd instructed Michael. After half an hour, he found himself back at the city park. He parked along the curb, and took a stroll. It was mostly empty at that hour, with only the occasional jogger or elderly person out for their morning walk. Donovan found a quiet spot near the fountain and took a seat.

He thought about Donna, about his job. He'd practically had an affair with Identinel for nine years, yet nothing good had come of it. Sure, he and Donna had their house and their car, but that was all. Their love for one another was the only thing Identinel hadn't paid for, but over the years Donovan's commitment to the company had put a strain on that love like nothing else. For that he could not forgive his employers, and he certainly could not forgive himself. Not only had he let Donna down, he'd let himself down as well.

He contemplated Dullington's question: *Who are* you*, Mr. Candle?*

Donovan realized he used to know. *Always wanted to be a writer*, he thought, as he idly plucked blades of grass from the earth, rolling them between his fingers before letting them fall. He'd discovered that desire for the written word during his college years, not long after meeting Donna, and it had been Chandler, King, and Koontz who had nurtured him through the early writing process. When one of his short stories took first place in his university's fiction contest, he knew in his heart that writing was what he wanted to do.

Back then, he'd had a plan: he'd get his degree, go to graduate school, marry Donna, write a bestseller, and support a family with his earnings. It wasn't until the end of school that he realized how fantastic it all seemed, and the bitter reality was that this lifestyle he dreamed of living was experienced by so very few. There were no ads in the newspaper reading "Seeking English Majors Fresh From College." With the job market in such a horrid state, Identinel had been his only choice.

Donovan remembered something else Dullington told him. He'd said it on Friday, when they first spoke on the phone at Identinel. *Actions breed definition.*

He thought about what he'd done to Sparrow, thought of the old man's accusing glare, and felt a twinge of guilt. The old man had caused to something to surface within Donovan, a violent urge to protect what he cared about, and the means to make a difficult decision when it had to be made. Knowing the kind of person Sparrow was made it easier to make some sort of peace with himself, though he feared what he'd done would come back to him, that he would have to answer for it.

When Joe Hopper, with his gruff, Southern drawl, spoke up, Donovan could almost smell the cigarettes on his breath. *He had it comin' to him, boss. You did the right thing. It's the rest of your life you should be concerned about.*

Donovan closed his eyes. What had he done to define himself?

As the world bustled on around him, Donovan realized he'd traded his dreams for dull reality that first day at Identinel. It hurt too badly to think about how much time he'd wasted there. *It's only temporary*, he'd said to himself as days turned to weeks, and so on. Time eroded, and soon he found himself ten pounds heavier. His hair was streaked with gray. The creativity upon which he'd once prided himself was all but gone. Joe Hopper had finally been born out of a last-ditch effort to prove to himself he could create.

And now that effort had died, just as empty as his own life.

Is this how I want to be remembered?

Donovan stood and brushed grass from his trousers. He stared up at the sky and the surrounding skyscrapers, then back down at the row of trees. The flickering reminded him of his brief chase through the Monochrome. As he walked to his car, he realized that Aleister Dullington's intervention in his life was, in some ways, a good thing. It was the wake-up call to his future happiness.

His father once told him that to betray oneself was the greatest sin of all, and to forgive oneself was the hardest thing to do. Donovan understood that now.

He started his car and pulled away from the curb. It was after ten on a beautiful Monday morning. *So this is what Mondays are* really *like*, he thought, smiling. He turned a corner onto another side-street and stepped on the gas. It was time to make his life pitch.

•

He drove back to Identinel, took the parking space closest to the building, and ran inside. Some of his coworkers acknowledged him, stopping to stare as he jogged across the foyer. Their notice was a sign that he was doing the right thing, and he could not hold back the huge grin on his face as he burst into Timothy Butler's office.

The Tammys sat across from Butler's desk, their mouths framed wide as they bickered about something. Butler, on the other hand, sat in his executive leather chair with his hands behind his head. All three were startled to see him. He stared at each one, focusing on their faces. The mere sight of them made his stomach churn, but he held his grin.

"Candle," Butler said, "what is—"

"My name is Donovan. If you call me Candle one more time, so help me, I'll cram a headset up your ass."

Fire and smoke spewed from his mouth. He could taste it on his lips. It made him ravenous for more.

"No one gives a shit about your stories, *Butler*. We don't care. Pay attention the next time you walk into the lounge. Everyone becomes suddenly occupied with other things for a reason, Tim. Think about that."

"Mr. Candle," Tammy Quilago snapped, "I think you're out of line—"

"Tammy," he said, still smiling, "shut your mouth."

Her face blossomed red. He watched it climb up her neck and flood her cheeks. Tammy Perpa started to chime in, but he held up a hand to silence her. The air was thick and hot. He hesitated for a moment, the smile pulling at his face. Two words perched at the tip of his tongue, where they'd been for the last nine years aching and waiting for their turn to be spoken. That time had finally come.

"I quit."

He turned and left the office. Outside, his coworkers peeked over their cubicles, headsets around their necks and eyes wide. *Now they can see me,* he thought. He was halfway to his desk when Butler and the Tammys emerged from the office. They walked toward the lounge and gave him grim, shocked glances.

As they passed by, Donovan experienced the gray sight for a brief interval. What he saw both frightened him and filled him with sick satisfaction. The three of them—Tammy Perpa, Tammy Quilago, and Timothy Butler—were fully visible, shimmering with the same sickening glow as Dr. Sparrow. He could see their wrinkles and graying hairs, their bad taste in clothing, and the frowns on their faces. Other people in the office appeared as dark phantoms with Cretins on their shoulders, and Donovan knew those creatures were not there for him. Not today. The Tammys and Timothy Butler would know a life transparent soon enough.

The office's color returned. Donovan chuckled to himself as he boxed up what little belongings he had. It was before noon on a Monday, and he was leaving Identinel a free man.

He did not look back.

•

He made one stop before returning home. The local animal shelter, where years before they'd adopted Mr. Precious Paws, was located not far from his neighborhood. He wandered between the rows of kennels and cages until his eye fell upon a tiny, orange ball of fur. When he leaned closer to the cage, two ears perked up, followed by two wide, green eyes. The tabby kitten purred.

A tag hanging from the wire mesh gave the feline's information. The owner had vanished, leaving behind a pregnant cat. This kitten was the only one of the litter to survive.

He smiled and poked his finger through the cage. The kitten pawed at it.

"I'll call you *Mrs.* Precious Paws," he whispered.

•

A few days later, Donovan received a phone call from his brother in the middle of dinner.

"Please don't answer that," she said. "Finish your meal."

He looked over, saw it was Michael's number on the ID, and winked at Donna. Any other time he would've let it ring, but he and his brother had grown close following their adventure. Donovan suspected Michael's call had something to do with his story, most likely about the role he had played in inspiring its character. *Maybe Joe Hopper was useful after all*, he thought, pressing the TALK button.

"Hello?"

"Hey, Don. What's going on?"

"Not much. Just having some dinner. You?"

"Ah, nothing really. Just finished up for the day." Michael paused for a moment, then spoke in a hushed tone. "I keep trying to remember what happened. And I know something happened, but it seems like each time I go back for a detail, it just isn't there."

Donovan closed his eyes. He'd experienced the same thing with Donna. Some details of the weekend remained, but others were lost to her, and Donovan didn't have the heart to fill them in. He preferred to be the only one to remember it all. For his wife and brother, some things were better left forgotten.

"It isn't important," he said, changing the subject. "Did you hear? I quit my job."

Michael's mood lightened. "I did. I'm really proud of you."

Donovan's cheeks flushed. "Thanks."

"No, I mean it. I know I don't say things like that very much, but yeah, I really mean it, Don. You really surprised me. I didn't think you would."

Donna finished her dinner, walked over, and kissed him on the cheek. Mrs. Precious Paws scampered after her, pawing at her ankles.

"And," Michael went on, "I'd like to offer you a job."

He felt a lump in his throat. "A job? Doing what?"

"Being my partner." An uncomfortable silence drifted across the line. Michael cleared his throat. "I mean, you've seen all the paperwork I have to deal with—"

Donovan laughed. "Me, a private investigator? You're serious?"

"Well, you'll have to be licensed first, but yeah, I'm serious. I figure it'll give you something to write about. And it's good job security, too, what with people disappearing left and right all the time."

The laugh they shared was a nervous one, but both knew the other meant well. Donovan accepted, and though the rest of the conversation whirled around the usual trivialities, he did not lose focus of his new prospect. Working with his brother seemed exciting, even validating, and when Donna later asked why he wore such a goofy smile, he could only say, "I'm going to work with my brother."

•

Donovan Candle experienced the flickering for the last time at 11:33 PM on a Saturday night. It had been two weeks since the incident, and the gray sight had become less frequent over time. The violent tugs at his stomach were reduced to vague tickling sensations, more uncomfortable than painful, and were so faint that he barely noticed them anymore.

He sat in his office staring at the blank computer screen. Over the last two weeks, he'd grown more as a person than at any other point in his life. If he'd done enough to remain in this reality, he and Donna would finally make their trip down to the shore for a weekend.

"Things," she'd told him, "always have a way of working out." He knew she was right. And somehow, as the days went on and the flickering decreased, he knew this was the case with his fate. Tonight, he sat down to begin the novel he'd put off for so long. It was his brother's encouragement that finally spurred him to action. Michael's job offer had started the wheels in his mind. *Together*, he thought, *we'll be Candle and Candle. Just like Holmes and Watson.*

He'd never seen himself as a detective, but after all that had happened, he realized it was just the kind of excitement he craved, even if reality couldn't match what he put to paper.

And so he'd wandered into the office after psyching himself up to face the interminable white space of his word processor. He sat down, pecked at the keys, and opened up the file for The Great American Novel.

He stared at the title and deleted it. *That's not right*, he thought. *There is no such thing.*

Instead he typed, "Monochrome Dream."

Just as he was about to jump to the next page, his vision went gray, and he felt the tickle of a hand around his gut. In the liminal space of his office, he saw the figure of Dr. Albert Sparrow. The old man shot an accusing gaze at Donovan, blaming him for his own actions, his own fate. Donovan no longer felt guilty. He stared back, shaking his head.

"I proved you wrong," he whispered.

The gray sight faded for the last time, and the tickle in his stomach ceased. For first time since that fateful Tuesday morning, he felt whole. But he did not dwell on it. Instead, he turned his attention back to the title.

"Monochrome Dream," he wrote, "by Donovan Candle."

He scrolled to the next page, a great white nothing daring him to act. He typed in italics, "For Donna," then sat back and smiled. Her love was all the meaning he would ever need, and it marked the perfect place to begin. Donovan heard Joe Hopper admonishing him from somewhere beyond the white space, in the depths of his head.

Get to it, boss.

Donovan put his fingers on the keys and began to write.

-ACKNOWLEDGMENTS-

This book has a weird history that goes back to 2006. It's a history about which I've written at length in other places, so I won't recount it here. It's been a long road, and there is a long list of people I need to thank. Many hands went into making this book happen, in its various forms, and I need to document them:

My undying thanks to my wife, Erica, for tolerating many late, lonely nights while I worked (and re-worked) this book. She kept me grounded when I needed to be, let me fly when there was no other option, and encouraged me when I didn't think I could go on. Thank you, Erica. You made me believe again.

Gratitude to my son, Gabriel, for teaching me that I have so much more to learn, and for inspiring me to reach for higher things greater than myself.

I owe most of this book to my editor, Amelia Snow, for taking on the project very late in the game, and believing in it. Her input made this book what it is, and her devotion to it did not waver. I think there were points at which she believed in it more than I did, and her belief helped pull me out of those poisonous doldrums as we raced for the finish line (even if we disagreed on the glass lenses).

Emma Fissenden worked under a ridiculous 48-hour window to film and produce this book's trailer. She was joined by Dan Goldberg behind the camera, and who lent his voice to the project. Travis Conrad Reichstein contributed his musical talents, composing "Monochrome for Piano in A Minor," giving the trailer (and the book) its own unique, classic sound. Sean Michael Errey portrayed Donovan Candle, and was joined by Brittney K. Robbins, Randy Nanjad, Emily Fister, Jillian Clair, and Raúl José on screen.

Tony Mahan, my best friend since junior high, lent his ear to many rants and raves about publishing, writing the book, and life in general. He also served as a technical advisor for the usage of firearms in this novel. The scene at the end of chapter five was plotted with enough trajectory detail to rival the research of the Warren Commission. If I got anything wrong, blame me.

Laura Lasky made it a point to check in on me every few weeks to make sure I was well, breathing, and of sound mind. I was usually two out of three.

My good friend Michael Lalonde kept me entertained with his comic, Orneryboy, and his girlfriend, Jennifer Krebsz, kept me clothed with the help of Sick On Sin.

Kelsey Desrosiers made me believe this story could be something more than a short story. It wouldn't be epic without her.

Cara Wallace provided crucial insight at the 11th hour, laying the foundation for the jacket copy which now exists on the cover.

Thanks are also in order for my writer friends present, absent, or departed: David Rockey, Phill English, Meg "Megatron" Finney, Bill Brown, Jon McRae, Steve Smith, Hope Fields, Henry Baum, Roxane Gay, Kirsty Logan, Tracy Lucas, Jenn Topper, Zoe Winters, Jessie Carty, Schuyler Towne, Thomas Purbrick, and Maija Haavisto.

My family and friends, who are too numerous to name here, dealt with my chronic absence from all manner of social events. They've offered various forms of support over the years, to which I am forever in their debt.

My coworkers at the "day job" have put up with my chronic sleep deprivation and pedantic tendencies for several years now, and there isn't a day that I don't appreciate their support and acceptance. Thanks Allan, Denise, Natascha, Steve, and Toni.

A trio of "super fans" have followed and supported this book since its original publication, and it would be a crime not to mention them here: Andrew Blemings, Matthew Rogers, and Eric Wiebe. Thanks, guys, for sticking with me after all this time. I hope you didn't cry foul at the changes this time around. I *know* you caught them.

Last, but certainly not least, the folks over at Kickstarter.com are due my eternal gratitude. They contributed to this project and made this definitive edition possible. They also paved the way for many more publishing adventures to come. Seriously, folks, without you, I wouldn't be writing this.

This last sentiment should be extended to you, dear Reader. Whether you're friend, family, Kickstarter backer, or a complete stranger—thank you for reading. I hope you enjoyed the book, and I hope to see you around next time.

Try not to flicker out before then.

Todd Keisling
Womelsdorf, PA
September 25th, 2006 – November 21st, 2010

-ABOUT THE AUTHOR-

Todd Keisling is a two-time recipient of the Oswald Research and Creativity Prize for fiction. His work has appeared in a number of print and online publications including *Limestone*, *Kaleidoscope*, and *365tomorrows*. Born in Kentucky, he now lives with his wife and son somewhere near Reading, Pennsylvania. Contrary to popular opinion, he *is* a cat person.

He loves hearing from readers. You can reach him by emailing todd@toddkeisling.com, or by following him on Twitter under the handle todd_keisling. He also welcomes patronage at his website, www.toddkeisling.com.